*Dane*

"I s...

Alex told Hank.

Every muscle in his body grew hard as he stared down at the extralarge piece of chocolate pie. Every time he thought he'd gotten past this stupid attraction that neither of them wanted, she went and did something like this.

It wasn't much, just a piece of pie. But it meant she thought about him, just like he thought about her. If only she knew what drove him downstairs in the middle of the night....

It was hunger, all right, but not the kind she meant, though he ended up trying to appease it with mere food. Knowing she'd heard him, that she'd lain awake while he stared at her closed door, sent heat shattering through him.

Dear Reader,

This month, Silhouette Romance unveils our newest promotion, VIRGIN BRIDES. This series, which celebrates first love, will feature original titles by some of Romance's best-loved stars, starting with perennial favorite Diana Palmer. In *The Princess Bride*, a feisty debutante sets her marriage sights on a hard-bitten, cynical cowboy. At first King Marshall resists, but when he realizes he may lose this innocent beauty—forever—he finds himself doing the unthinkable: proposing.

Stranded together in a secluded cabin, single mom and marked woman Madison Delaney finds comfort—and love—in *In Care of the Sheriff*, this month's FABULOUS FATHERS title, as well as the first book of Susan Meier's new miniseries, TEXAS FAMILY TIES. Donna Clayton's miniseries MOTHER & CHILD also debuts with *The Stand-by Significant Other*. A workaholic businesswoman accepts her teenage daughter's challenge to "get a life," but she quickly discovers that safe—but irresistibly sexy—suitor Ryan Shane is playing havoc with her heart.

In Laura Anthony's compelling new title, *Bride of a Texas Trueblood*, Deannie Hollis would do *anything* to win back her family homestead—even marry the son of her enemy. In Elizabeth Harbison's sassy story, *Two Brothers and a Bride*, diner waitress Joleen Wheeler finds herself falling for the black-sheep brother of her soon-to-be fiancé.... Finally, Martha Shields tells a heartwarming tale about a woman's quest for a haven and the strong, silent rancher who shows her that *Home is Where Hank is*.

In April and May, look for VIRGIN BRIDES titles by Elizabeth August and Annette Broadrick. And enjoy each and every emotional, heartwarming story to be found in a Silhouette Romance.

Regards,

*Joan Marlow Golan*

Joan Marlow Golan
Senior Editor Silhouette Books

---

Please address questions and book requests to:
Silhouette Reader Service
U.S.: 3010 Walden Ave., P.O. Box 1325, Buffalo, NY 14269
Canadian: P.O. Box 609, Fort Erie, Ont. L2A 5X3

# HOME IS WHERE HANK IS

## Martha Shields

Silhouette
R O M A N C E™
Published by Silhouette Books
America's Publisher of Contemporary Romance

Dedicated to my parents, Lu and J. C. Townsend, who
always believed in me and my stories.

Acknowledgments

I'd like to thank the chamber of commerce in Dubois,
Wyoming, for all the information they sent about the
area, and Sylvia Crouter of the Box Hanging Three
Ranch for patiently answering all my questions about
ranch life in the Wind River Valley.

 SILHOUETTE BOOKS

ISBN 0-373-19287-8

HOME IS WHERE HANK IS

Copyright © 1998 by Martha Shields

## MARTHA SHIELDS

grew up telling stories to her sister to pass the time on the long drives to their grandparents' house. Since she's never been able to stop dreaming up characters, she's happy to be able to share her stories with a wider audience. Martha lives in Memphis, Tennessee, with her husband, teenage daughter and a cairn "terror" who keeps trying to live up to his Toto ancestry. Martha has a master's degree in journalism and works at a local university.

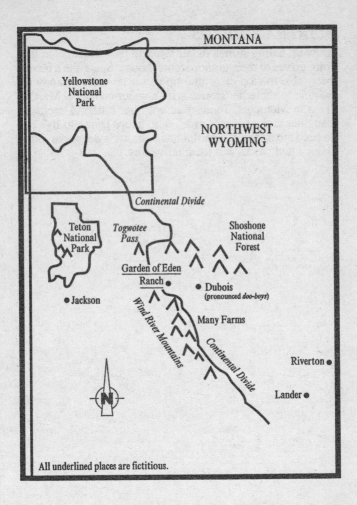

All underlined places are fictitious.

# *Chapter One*

Hank Eden closed his eyes as the tart sweetness of lemon icebox pie slid into his mouth. If his sister could cook this well, he would never have had to leave the ranch on a perfectly good working day.

Not even the rattle of a tray filled with dishes could distract him.

"You look like a man who's enjoying hisself."

He opened one eye to see Henrietta Gibbs's ample bosom leaning over the back of the next booth. Her round face was painted to perfection—he'd never seen one inch of real skin above her neck. Her hennaed hair was piled on top of her head in curled contortions held in place with liquid-armor-in-a-can.

Hank swallowed reluctantly, and the last bite slid down his throat. "Damn, Hen. When did Butch learn to cook?"

The owner of the Whiskey Mountain Café released a laugh that sounded like the bark of one of Hank's blue heeler dogs. "You don't really think my old man made that pie, do ya? He can't cook nothing that don't have beans in it." Hen raised her voice so her husband would be sure to hear.

Hen and Butch's lighthearted feud was a running joke at the café, but it was their spats as much as Butch's four-alarm chili that kept the folks in Dubois, Wyoming, coming back decade after decade.

Hank's eyes narrowed. "Don't tell me you made this pie."

Henrietta flopped one hand at him and ambled over to run her rag over an already-clean table. "You got beans in your head? You know Butch don't allow me in his kitchen 'cept to pick up orders. I work the front, he works the back. That's the way we both like it. Ain't likely to change after thirty years."

"Then who—"

"Alex made them pies."

Hank peered around Henrietta's ample figure. "There's more?"

She barked another laugh. "There was this morning. Apple, cherry, coconut custard—"

"All as good as this?"

"Every bite."

"I'd like to meet this fellow. He anywhere around? I don't suppose he—"

"Whoa, cowboy. Alex ain't no fella. She's female."

"Female? Did you say Alice or Alex?"

"Alex. For Alexandra. Last name's Miller. Zeke towed her and her car in last Thursday. A heap of junk, if you ask me. And I seen some junk heaps in my day. Foreign job. Sorry thing broke down just this side of the reservation."

"So you hired her?"

"Not really. Can't afford any more help. You know that. There's not enough work around here for me, not till summer tourist season. Poor thing's just working for tips, trying to earn enough to get her car fixed."

"She looking for a job?" Hank asked.

"You got one?"

"I do if she can cook everything half as good as that pie. Mrs. Johnson quit. Couldn't stand living so far from her grand-babies since her boy moved down to Texas. We've been eating Claire's cooking for the past two weeks." He grimaced as he remembered last night's supper. "My men are threatening to quit if I don't find someone who can at least make a decent pot of coffee. You know how much good grub means to cowboys."

Henrietta heaved a sigh and plopped down in a chair. "I can't vouch for nothing but the pies. You know how Butch is about his kitchen. The only reason she's allowed to make the pies is that she got here earlier than Butch one morning before she knew any better. Poor thing. Thought she was helping out. Didn't deserve the blessing-out Butch gave her 'fore he tasted that pie. After he did, he couldn't say no to her."

"But can she cook anything else?"

"She claims to be a cook, and I believe her. Crust like that only comes from them that knows their way around a kitchen. She was headed for California when she got stuck here. Gonna study under some chef at one of them hoity-toity restaurants that serve white goop all over everything."

"Where she staying?"

"I talked Henry into letting her have a special rate down at the Horse Creek Motel. Even so, she's barely making enough to cover a room."

Hank's brow lifted. "She's that bad off? Where's she from?"

"Alabama is all I know, and that only 'cause I had to know where she got that accent."

He nodded. The Code of the West had always forbade delving into a person's past, and that code still held. But Wyoming was a long way from Alabama, and he wondered how she wound up here. "I wonder if she—"

"Hen! You here?"

The female voice came from the kitchen, and both heads swiveled toward the swinging door. Hank could hear Butch saying where to find Henrietta.

"That's her," Henrietta told him, then raised her voice. "Come on in here, Alex. I got somebody that wants to meet you."

The door swung out, and Hank's first impression was a pair of legs that reached from the floor to heaven. His widening eyes followed the faded, form-fitting jeans to gently flaring hips. Above the jeans he couldn't tell much because an oversize denim jacket on top of a flannel shirt hid her from the hips up. Telling himself it was ridiculous to feel cheated, Hank noted the binoculars hanging around her neck before meeting a pair of golden-hazel eyes that regarded him suspiciously.

He blinked. "You're just a kid!"

Alex stiffened. "Nice to meet you, too, mister." She spun on her heel and headed back into the kitchen.

"No, wait!" He rose to his feet as she stopped and looked at him over her shoulder. "I'm sorry. You're just so young."

Her thick mass of deep brown hair—tied back with a blue rubber band—gleamed with rich red highlights in the dim light of the café. It fell halfway to her waist, and Hank had to drag his mind back from wondering what it would feel like spilling over his bare chest. Hell, he couldn't hire this woman. If he were reacting like a randy jackrabbit, every unattached cowboy in the Wind River Valley would be hanging around his back door. And the three single hands he had wouldn't be able to keep their minds on business.

Her chin lifted a notch. "I'm twenty-five, if it's any of your business."

Henrietta cleared her throat. "Alex, this here's Hank Eden. He usually ain't this rude. He needs a cook out at his ranch. You interested in helping him out for a while?"

The golden-brown eyes traveled down his frame, as if assessing his worth—both as a man and a boss. Though secure in his abilities at each, Hank had to steel himself to keep from squirming under her perusal.

"How much does it pay?" she said at last. She drew out the words, and for the first time Hank noticed her deep Southern accent. Her voice flowed over him like warm honey.

Hank surprised himself by suggesting a ridiculously low amount of money.

"I may be young, Mr. Eden, but I'm not stupid." Alex turned to walk through the kitchen door. A few seconds later he heard the back door open and slam closed.

He watched the kitchen door until it stopped swinging. He'd panicked. Gut feeling told him Alexandra Miller was trouble. He'd never reacted to a woman so strongly. He'd never wanted to drag a woman who hadn't uttered twenty words in his presence to the nearest bed. Until today.

"If your momma was alive, she'd whup your butt all the way to the Idaho line. Why in tarnation were you so rude?"

He turned to see Hen's incredulous face, then lifted his hat and plowed a hand through his hair. "I don't know."

"You want a cook, don't you?"

He took a deep breath and released it as he sank into the padded booth. "I've got to have one. We'll starve on Claire's cooking."

"I don't know nobody else around these parts looking for a cooking job, do you?"

"No."

Hen threw up her hands. "Are you crazy or something? You all but dared her to take the job. Look, Hank, she ain't no buckle chaser, if that's what's got you worried. Matter of fact, she's on the shy side. A couple of cowboys were in here the other day, hittin' on her, and she hid out in the kitchen with Butch."

Hank had a sudden urge to ask Hen who those cowboys were so he could do some hitting himself. But he didn't voice it. How the hell could he feel so protective toward a woman he didn't even know? A jaw muscle twitched in frustration. "She's too young."

Hen snorted. "Pots and pans don't care how old you are. 'Sides, you were a year younger than her when you took over operations at the Garden."

"That's different. When Dad and Momma died Travis was only fourteen and Claire—besides being a girl—was only nine. There was no one else to do it."

"Just like there's no one else around to be your cook. God sent her here just when you needed her. You gonna turn your back on that?"

Hank stared blindly at a taped-over vinyl patch on the booth's other side. Hen was right. He had to hire this young woman. Whether God or fate or the two combined had a hand in it, she was a cook and she was right where he needed her when he needed her. The only other choice was to put an advertisement in the newspaper and wait until someone else responded. That could take weeks. As it was, he was only going to need a cook for a few months, if all went according to plan. He hated hiring someone for such a short time, especially when he couldn't tell them the job wasn't permanent. But he had to have a cook. If he didn't his belt buckle would soon be rattling against his backbone, and his ranch hands would all quit.

Henrietta rose as a customer came in. Hank's gaze shifted to the kitchen door. When he first laid eyes on Alex, he'd felt like a lassoed calf—all tied up—when he just wanted to get the hell out of there.

He'd been biding his time for eight years, waiting for his younger brother and sister to grow up. Travis finished high school four years ago, and Claire would graduate in May. He could finally see the light at the end of the lasso. The last thing he needed was another rope tying him to the Garden.

Muttering a curse, he shook his head to clear it.

Alex Miller was a woman, just like any other. He needed a cook and she could cook. That's *all* he needed. As long as he remembered that, he'd be okay.

"Any idea where she went?" he asked as Henrietta walked past him.

"Shouldn't be too far out back. Likes to watch for critters with Butch's glasses." Hen opened the kitchen door with her rear end and sang out to her husband, "Wake up, honey."

Hank stood and threw down more than enough cash to cover the pie and coffee. He nodded to the other customer, a newcomer to Dubois whom he'd met but didn't know well, then grabbed his coat and headed out the door.

A shrill whistle led him around to the back of the café. Alex sat on the lowered tail of Butch's truck, patting her thighs to urge Butch's Labrador over. The big black dog tore across the yard, eager to have her attention.

Though she didn't look at him directly, Hank knew the instant she became aware of his approach. She went still for a split second, then lifted Butch's binoculars and trained them on Whiskey Mountain.

His boots crunched through the gravel, but she didn't move when he walked up and sat next to her, the truck dipping under his weight.

"You'll get a better view of the sheep in the summer," he said. "We've got the largest herd of bighorns in North America. Nearly a thousand."

"Hen told me."

"They built a national center here that tells about the sheep. They've got a mountain in the middle of it with little figures of—"

"I went there day before yesterday."

"Oh." Hank scanned Whiskey Mountain. His sharp eyes could barely make out movement about halfway up the side. "Well, how was it? I haven't been yet."

Her mouth quirked and the binoculars dipped slightly, but she said nothing.

"Look, I'm sorry about what I said in there. It's just that every cook I've hired has been old enough to be my mother. You took me by surprise."

Slowly she lowered the binoculars and turned her head to study his face. In the sunlight her eyes were molten gold. Their flickering fires fascinated him.

Finally she said, "Forget it."

"I'd like to start over, if that's okay. You know, get off on the right foot this time." Though she didn't move, Hank saw her eyes glaze over, the gold suddenly tarnished. "Something wrong?"

"I'm sorry. I can't be your cook. I've got a job. Well, not a job, really, more of an internship. I'm going to study under Etienne Buchaude."

The reverence in her voice spoke volumes. "He's a good cook, is he?"

Her eyes widened at his careless observation. "Cook? Monsieur Buchaude is one of the greatest *chefs* in the country."

Enjoying her pique, he pushed further. "What's the difference?"

"Cooks prepare food. I am a mere cook. Monsieur Buchaude is an artist."

"You mean those fancy sauces and flowers on the plate?" Hank snorted. "Give me a cook anyday. Like you."

She evidently realized which path he was leading the conversation down because she leaned back and shook her head. "I can't."

Hank cursed under his breath and looked away. So much for subtlety. What now? Put an ad in the paper and cross his fingers? What if his men quit? Where would he be then? Good ranch hands weren't easy to come by these days, not around Dubois. They'd all moved to parts of Wyoming where ranches weren't being taxed out of existence.

The beef industry in the Wind River Valley had all but dried up since they'd become "Jacksonized." Like in nearby Jackson Hole, ranch land was being converted into condos for wealthy retirees and movie stars. Property taxes had escalated at a rate that put most ranches out of business.

Hank was barely holding on to the Garden. He couldn't hold on much longer. That was one reason he'd put his ranch up for sale last month. The agent told him it would be a couple of months before they got any serious offers. So until then he needed hands to work his cattle, which meant he needed a cook, which meant he needed Alex.

"Look, I don't mean to pry, but how are you planning to get to California? Hen told me your car broke down and you don't have the money to fix it."

Her firm little chin lifted. "Hen talks too much."

"I can't disagree with you there. But that doesn't change the fact that you need a job. Unless what you're looking for is a handout...."

She straightened indignantly. "I don't take charity."

He nodded in approval. "Do you take jobs?"

Alex released a huff of breath and looked away. Damn the man. He had her there. How was she going to get to San Francisco? The pittance she made at the Whiskey Mountain Café barely paid for her room. She hadn't panicked yet because her internship didn't actually start for another month. Etienne's was only open during the summer and winter tourist seasons. Monsieur Buchaude made enough money during those seven months to live the rest of the year in the south of France. She'd been planning to get a part-time job in one of the many hotels or restaurants in San Francisco until Etienne's opened. She just hadn't counted on her car breaking down.

She threw a glance at the man sitting next to her. He studied her with a strange expression—as if he couldn't quite figure out what species she was. His perusal reminded her of when she answered Hen's call and first walked through that door to find his startling blue eyes on her. She couldn't understand how he ripped the breath right out of her lungs. She knew it had to be her imagination, but she'd actually felt his gaze on her—like hands wandering up her body.

Alex shivered. Men had looked her over before, but it usually made her feel dirty. She'd never felt her skin tingle in response, as if every hair on her body was clamoring for attention. Her heart had never hammered blood through her veins until she felt light-headed.

Feeling those bright blue eyes on her now, she felt those symptoms return. How could she work for this man when her hands shook every time he looked at her? She'd break every dish in his kitchen.

"So, how about it?" he asked. "I won't ask for a lifetime commitment. If you could just help me out for a few weeks, I'd be eternally grateful."

He named a much more reasonable salary. If she worked a month for him, she'd be able to fix her car, drive to San Francisco and have a bit left to tide her over until she got settled. Why not take his offer? She had to have some kind of job for the next month. Wyoming or California—what difference did it make?

She forced her eyes back to him. The curved brim of his black hat threw shadows across his features, making them look as if they had been chiseled or hewn. His eyes were the same color as the Wyoming sky.

Alex couldn't squelch the warm pleasure the look in those eyes sent seeping through her, melting her bones—which told her exactly why she shouldn't take this job. The last thing she needed right now was a hot romance with some cowboy. The chance of a lifetime waited for her in California. No way was she passing that up.

But she had to face facts. She needed this job in order to get to California.

She took a deep breath and shook away her misgivings. She really needed to get out more. This man hadn't asked for anything more than a cook. One smile and her underused libido ran amok. "You own a ranch?"

He nodded. "About ten miles west of here."

"What's the name of it?"

"Most folks call it the Garden."

Alex felt her lips twitch. "As in the Garden of Eden?"

He nodded, acknowledging the joke. "My great-granddaddy named it. Came with the last name, I guess. He even went so far as to make our cattle brand a snake."

Alex chuckled and felt herself relax. At least he had a sense of humor. "Seems appropriate."

"I reckon."

The dog nudged Alex's leg and she leaned over to scratch behind his ears.

"Tell me, is everything you cook as good as that lemon pie?" he asked.

"You liked it?"

"Does a cowboy like steak? Does a horse like carrots? Does a cat like—"

"I get the idea." She smiled broadly. "And to answer your question—yes, I'm a very good cook."

"You interested in the job?"

"Maybe. How many people would I be cooking for?"

"Let's see, there's me and my sister Claire. I've got five full-time hands, but two are married and have their own places on the ranch. So that leaves Jed, Derek and Buck. Oh, and my brother, Travis, drifts in from time to time. He may show up while you're there. Think you can handle a crowd like that? We're all big eaters. All except Claire."

The more the better, as far as Alex was concerned. Cooking for four hungry men would take a lot of time. Time that couldn't be spent thinking about blue eyes and broad shoulders. "How old is your sister?"

"Seventeen. She's graduating from high school this year."

"And she can't cook?"

He grimaced. "About as well as a black Angus bull can fly."

Alex smiled at the image. "Maybe I can teach her a thing or two."

"Then you'll take the job?"

She thrust her hand toward him before she could change her mind. The jolt that shot up her arm when his warm fingers closed around hers made her blink. She had to clear the sudden huskiness from her throat before she managed, "Yes, Mr. Eden, I'll take your job." *And hope I don't regret it.*

The bright yellow VW bug that Alex had nicknamed Sunshine rattled and bumped along the gravel road. When the front wheel dipped into a deep rut, Sugar yowled. Alex took one hand from the wheel to rub the orange-red fur of the large feline.

"I know, Sugar. I was thinking the same thing. What have I gotten us into now? If Sunshine was a bucket of bolts before, she's going to be a bucket of loose bolts by the time we get there." She patted the dashboard. "If ever a road was made for a four-wheeler, we've found it.

"This has to be the right road, Sugar. He said the third turnoff to the left. Be patient. He said it was 'a good ways,' but I've got a sneaking suspicion that 'a good ways' in Wyoming is not the same as 'a good ways' in Alabama."

From the highway, she'd turned from the narrow Wind River Valley that sheltered Dubois up into hills timbered with pines and aspens. The country was as different from her Alabama home as a pot roast cooked in a Dutch oven was different from one cooked on a rack. One was closed in, the other wide open. One was moist and tender, the other dry and sometimes tough.

During the months she'd spent out West—first in Colorado, then Wyoming—she'd discovered that in some ways she liked the wide-open spaces. From the front door of her Dubois motel room, she could see mountains in all directions. The sky at night stole her breath away. Some nights she felt that if she reached up a hand, she could pluck a star right from the velvety darkness. The vastness made her feel humble…and more alone than ever. That's the part she didn't like.

Alex had been alone most of her life. Even though surrounded by other children at the orphanage in LaNett, Alabama, she'd never fit in. She'd never had a best friend. The girls at the orphanage came and went—some were adopted, some were taken in by relatives, some were taken to foster homes by the state.

The sisters who ran the orphanage tried to make her feel special, feel wanted, but they had over fifty kids to deal with on a daily basis. Alex had come to the orphanage at the advanced age of eight, after caring for her mother through an endless year of bronchitis and pneumonia until her death, so her needs were often overlooked for those of the younger, less self-sufficient children. Alex helped when she could, but when the children she tended were taken away from the orphanage, she felt abandoned, alone, unwanted. Eventually she'd retreated to the orphanage kitchen, where they were glad to have her eager help. Only there did she feel useful, feel wanted.

"But I've got you now, Sugar. You won't leave me, right?" As she petted the thick ginger fur, the cat's slanted green eyes blinked at her. "That reminds me. I didn't tell Mr. Eden I have a cat. Hope he doesn't mind."

Alex smiled when Sugar meowed, as if objecting to the fact that he might not be wanted. "Don't worry. If you go, I go. And he seemed pretty desperate for a cook. Now if we could only find the place…."

Half a mile later, Alex stopped as the rocky road took a sharp right. Just on the other side of a flat, railingless bridge stood the standard ranch entrance. The split-rail fence she'd followed for the past mile rose into hand-hewn posts to form a frame for the gate. Iron letters proclaimed this land "The Garden of Eden." A crude representation of a snake—a squiggly line with an oval on one end—curled away in opposite directions on either side of the name.

"Sure isn't what I imagined the Garden of Eden looking like. I mean, it's not bad, there just aren't any apple trees."

Alex smiled at her joke, wrestled with the stick shift until it ground into first, then lurched across the bridge and over the cattle guard under the sign. Half a mile later, just as she crested a hill, she came to a gate.

Slowing to a halt, she stared at it. "I don't see a house yet. You think it's okay to just open it and go through?"

The cat stared at the gate just as intently as Alex, then growled an echo of his mistress's confusion.

Alex stroked his head. "I guess we don't have much choice, do we? Tell you what. I'll open the gate, you drive through, okay?"

She laughed as the cat blinked at her, then she climbed from the car. The gate swung open easily on well-oiled hinges. Alex ran back, jumped in the car, pulled through, then climbed out again to close it. She had to repeat this process two more times before she rounded a sharp bend and heard a faint call.

She swiveled her head until she finally spotted her new boss galloping up on the right side of the car. She slowed to a stop and leaned over to roll down the window.

He rode like he was born in a saddle, easily controlling the black mare beneath him. A denim jacket stretched across his broad shoulders, which angled down to lean hips encased in faded jeans. With his black hat and well-worn boots, he could've been the ghost of a cowboy from a century ago.

But Alex knew the difference. Back at the café she'd felt Butch's truck dip under Hank Eden's weight as he'd sat beside her on the tailgate, and she'd felt his broad shoulders nudge her over to make room. She'd felt the warmth he gave off, like a pie just out of the oven. This was no specter of the range coming at her, but a flesh-and-blood cowboy. And just like cowgirls of old, her heart raced like the horse under his saddle.

She shivered as she caught a glimpse of faded jeans stretching across a small, tight rear end when he dismounted. Though she'd just met him a couple of days before, it seemed as if she'd known this man all her life.

Hank looked over the squatty, bright yellow car as he rode up and dismounted. Boxes and bags filled the tiny back seat, and a one-eared cat peered at him out the front window.

Pushing his hat back on his head, he leaned over. The same golden eyes that haunted his dreams the past two nights watched him warily.

"Hi! Glad to see I'm on the right road," she drawled.

Hank nodded. "Howdy. I'm surprised to see you here so soon. Thought it'd be tomorrow at best."

She shook her head, sending waves of afternoon light dancing down her unbound hair. "Zeke had already ordered the part. I came as soon as he tightened the last bolt." She glanced down, then back up. "Thanks for advancing me enough money to get my car fixed."

He shrugged. "Hate to see a body stuck out here without a way into town. 'Sides, you'll work it off."

"How did you know I wouldn't just drive on to California?"

"Were you planning on it?"

"No, but I could have."

"No sense fretting about what didn't happen. There's enough to worry about with what does." He scanned the contents of her car. "This everything?"

She nodded. "It's everything I own."

Before he could comment, the cat meowed. Alex reached out to rub its head. "I forgot to tell you I have a cat. I hope you don't mind. He's a house cat, but he's very clean."

"He a good mouser?"

"Oh, yes. He's had to be, at some of the places we've stayed."

Hank searched her eyes, but she didn't seem to be complaining, just stating fact. "Then he's welcome."

Her chest collapsed with relief. "Thanks."

"Any more surprises?"

"No."

"Fine. You're about half a mile from the house. Make yourself at home. Claire'll be home from school soon. I'd go in with you, but I was on the trail of some strays when I saw the dust your car stirred up. Don't want to lose them."

"You go ahead. Don't worry about us. We'll be fine."

He nodded, then pointed up the road. "You can't miss it."

"Thanks, see you later."

Hank stepped away and winced as the car ground into gear. The worn tires kicked up a few rocks, making his mount shy back, but Hank held on to the reins easily, his attention staying on the bright yellow heap as it clambered over the hill.

The feeling that had punched him in the gut the first time he'd laid eyes on her—the feeling that he'd met his fate head-on—came back even stronger than before. She'd been on his mind ever since he'd hired her. He'd told himself he should ride back into town and call the whole thing off, but he hadn't. He needed a cook.

He tore his gaze from the settling dust, mounted and turned his horse around. The only reason he hired her was to cook. The only reason he suddenly looked forward to going home that night—after so many years of not giving a hoot in hell one way or the other—was so he could sink his teeth into a plate of decent food.

Maybe if he repeated those words often enough, he'd believe it.

Sunshine rolled to a stop in front of the last gate, which sat about fifty yards from the house, but Alex barely saw the barrier. Her eyes never left the compound tucked away in a small, wooded valley as she slowly climbed from the car and leaned against the wooden gate.

In the midst of several flat, dark buildings rose a two-story house with a steep-pitched roof. Surrounded by mountains, it sat against a backdrop of timbered peaks. By far one of the largest and oldest houses she'd seen around Dubois, it brought to mind the image of an old Victorian lady who sat sedately in her well-worn, threadbare finery.

The once-white clapboards needed a coat of paint. Dirt covered the wide porch that spanned the front. The flower beds hadn't been tended in who knew how many years, and a shutter on an upstairs window hung askew.

This home needed someone.

Unbidden, a day at the orphanage floated across Alex's mind, as clear as if it happened last week. A little girl whom she'd cared for like a mother for over a year had been adopted. Alex still remembered how bereft she felt as she stood at an upstairs window, watching the little girl being carried away in her new daddy's arms. Tears had streamed down her face, and silent sobs had racked her body as they drove away. She knew she'd never see little Becky again.

Sister Mary Clara found her there and tried to give what comfort she could. "Somewhere in the world is a home for every single person," the nun had said. "Just be patient, work hard and you'll find your home. You'll see."

She hadn't thought about that incident in eons. Why would she remember it now?

A loud, complaining yowl broke into her thoughts. Sugar was getting impatient. Opening the gate, Alex returned to the car. Her eyes fell on the house again.

Six years had passed since the orphanage had shut down and she'd been forced to leave the cooking job they'd given her after she turned eighteen. Suddenly Alex realized that during all those years spent drifting from town to town, job to job, she'd been looking for her home, a place that needed her. Not a place that hired her as one of several cooks or waitresses. Not a place that felt sorry for her because her car broke down and she didn't have the money to fix it. A place that needed her. A place she could call home.

Stunned and a bit frightened, she shook her head vehemently. The Garden of Eden was *not* that place. She was here for one month, that's all. She had plans, and they did not include a broken-down old house and a cowboy with hungry eyes.

If she'd learned anything the past few years it was that life didn't hand you anything. You had to work, and work hard, for every scrap you got. She was tired of bouncing around hoping to land in the spot where she belonged. She was going to make her own home. After learning all she could from Monsieur Buchaude, she was going to open her own restaurant.

Alex loved to cook; had, ever since her mother had first sat her on the counter when she was six and let her stir the soup. Though it had become a necessity instead of playtime—first when her mother got sick, then helping out at the orphanage—she still loved to create good things that people enjoyed eating.

She hadn't decided exactly where to open her restaurant, but it would be her home and her customers would be her family.

Alex wrestled the car into first gear. 'Life on the road must be getting to me, Sugar. I'm beginning to hallucinate. This is just a ranch that's seen better days. It's not our home.''

As she rolled up to the house however, she couldn't shake the feeling that the grand old lady was opening her arms in welcome.

## Chapter Two

Even though the house beckoned, Alex was reluctant to enter with no one home. So she made a circuit of the ranch buildings.

Just after she returned to the car and pulled Sugar out, she heard the unmistakable sound of a vehicle coming down the drive. She ran to open the gate with the cat in her arms. A battered black truck came barreling down the drive and screeched to a halt at the open gate.

A young woman stuck her head out the window. Her straight, dark brown hair was pulled back into a thick braid, and her deep blue eyes were wide. "You can't be the new cook! You're not supposed to be here until tomorrow."

Alex blinked at the shocked tone. "I came as soon as Zeke fixed my car. Am I too early?"

"I'll say! I didn't have a chance to clean up the dishes from breakfast before I left for school." The girl pushed back a strand of hair that escaped her braid and looked Alex over. "Besides, you're not any older than I am."

"I'm eight years older than you, if you're Claire."

"Oh, I'm not disappointed. I'm thrilled! It's just that I was expecting another one like Mrs. Johnson."

"Is that bad?"

The young woman rolled her eyes. "Come on. I'll ride you to the house."

"That's all right, I can wal—"

The truck took off, leaving Alex's words in the dust. It slammed to a stop on the other side of the gate, so Alex swung the gate shut and climbed in.

"You are Claire, right?" Alex said as the truck sped down the drive.

The girl threw her a sheepish look. "Sorry. I was so surprised I forgot my manners. Yeah, I'm Claire Eden, and I sure am glad to see you, even if you're only going to be here a month."

"Because I can cook?"

Claire smiled easily. "Well, that's a big part of it. I hate to cook worse than the boys hate to eat what I cook. But it's more than that."

"Oh? What?" Alex held on to Sugar with both hands as Claire barreled around the house. She closed her eyes, certain they would go straight through the other side of the garage. As they skidded to a stop, Alex stiffened her feet against the floorboard to keep from flying through the windshield. Slitting one eye, she peeked around nervously. The front bumper couldn't be more than a few inches from the back wall.

Claire stared thoughtfully at the wheel as if nothing unusual had happened. "Hank's hiring you means he finally realizes I'm grown up. All the others were part cook and part baby-sitter."

"All the others?" Alex repeated. "How many were there?"

"Eight." Claire gathered her books from the seat between them. "You're the ninth cook we've had in eight years. That's a beautiful cat. What happened to its ear?"

"I don't know. It was already gone when I found him," she replied absently. *Eight cooks!* What had she gotten herself into?

"Can I pet him?"

"Sure. Sugar's a good cat."

Claire rubbed Sugar's head, then opened her door and set

off for the house. "Come on, I'll show you where to put your stuff."

"Why eight cooks?" Alex asked as she followed Claire up the steps. This porch mirrored the one on the front of the house, except for a swing at one end.

Her hand on the screen door, Claire turned to look at Alex. A frown drew her brows together, and she shook her head. "I don't want to scare you away."

"Is the house haunted or something?"

Claire smiled wryly. "Let's just say that when we sit down to supper tonight, the words *pig trough* will probably cross your mind."

The kitchen window had a perfect view of the main barn, a detail Alex suspected one of the Eden wives had planned carefully. She knew exactly when the men rode in that evening. The three single hands rode more or less abreast, laughing and joking. Hank came in ten minutes later.

A shiver of anticipation skimmed over her skin.

Appalled by this reaction, she turned away from the window and grabbed a heavy stoneware pitcher. She filled the pitcher with cold water, then strained the steeped tea into it. As she poured it into six goblets, Claire pushed open the door from the dining room.

"Are you out of your mind?"

Alex's eyes grew wide. They'd had a nice long talk that afternoon while Claire showed her around the house. Alex thought they were well on their way to becoming friends, so she asked with trepidation, "What?"

"Grandma's china and a linen table cloth? For cowboys?"

"That's bad?"

"It is for these cowboys. Come on, we have to change everything fast."

Alex threw a look out the kitchen window. She didn't see anyone heading toward the house yet, so she hurried into the dining room.

"I was just trying to dress things up a little." She scraped all the silver together as Claire stacked the dishes. "I didn't mean to hurt anything."

"I know. I should've warned you earlier. These guys descend on a table like a plague of locusts."

They had everything put away and earthenware plates around the table by the time the back door creaked open.

"Ouuu-weee! Don't that smell good?"

"Sure does. I'll bet my silver spurs our new cook rode in today."

"Hell, Jed. That ain't no bet. You could tell it ain't Claire's cookin' cause there ain't no smoke floating out the door."

Alex threw Claire a sympathetic glance, but the girl just shrugged, picked up the large bowl of mashed potatoes and pushed her way into the dining room. Alex followed with a plate of biscuits. She set them on the table, then turned to greet the hands who stomped noisily down the hall.

She smelled them before she saw them. The acrid scent of sweat mixed with the earthy odors of manure and dirt drifted in ahead of three cowboys. Alex flexed the fingers that wanted to scratch her nose as they filled the doorway. Stair-stepped in height, they all wore jeans showing a thick coating of dust and hats that threw their faces into shadow. Long-sleeved Western-style shirts showed stains of sweat, and boots caked with dirt still had spurs attached.

The three stopped as one and stared at her as if they saw a ghost. Alex stared back, wondering if they were the Three Stooges or the Three Musketeers.

"This here's the new cook, boys," Claire told them. "Alexandra Miller."

"Hey," she said nervously. "Y'all call me Alex."

"What's the matter, boys?" Claire taunted. "Cat got your tongues?"

The shortest cowboy recovered first. With black eyes and sandy blond hair that stuck out at odd angles, he came forward and tipped his hat. "Howdy, ma'am. I'm Buck. I don't know what sight's purtier, you or that plate of steaks."

The tallest came next. Skinny as the railings supporting the banister, with a large nose and a prominent Adam's apple bobbing in his neck, he resembled the image Alex had always had of Ichabod Crane.

"I'm Jed. Pleased to meet ya."

"I'm Derek," the next one said. Though not the tallest, his black hair and mustache, coupled with green eyes, would make him stand out in any crowd. "The boss sure pulled one over on us this time. We thought you was a heifer like the last— oops, pardon me, ma'am. Don't mean to speak ill of the departed."

"The last cook *died?*" Alex asked in alarm.

Claire glared at Derek. "Of course not. She moved to Texas to be with her grandbabies."

He grinned. "Well, she departed, didn't she?"

The atmosphere suddenly changed, and Alex knew before she turned that Hank stood in the doorway. She had the same sensation she'd had at the café and in her car. Electricity surged from him. It flowed around her like an aura, making her skin tingle. She turned to find his eyes on her.

Had she thought Derek handsome? That cowboy faded into the yellowed wallpaper when Hank walked into the room.

"'Bout time you made it in, boss," Derek complained. "We're starving."

Claire poked Derek as she walked to her chair. "You're always starving."

"That's right, little filly. Starving for you." Derek shot out an arm to capture her waist, but Claire eluded him.

"But not my cooking."

He grinned and pulled out her chair. "That don't matter. I can cook."

"What, beans?"

He sat in the chair next to her. "Any way you like 'em."

The other hands took the chairs across the table, but Hank paid them no mind. His attention stayed on a pair of golden-brown eyes that wouldn't let go of his. He'd seen this woman a total of two times and already she seemed familiar. She'd bound her chestnut hair with a rubber band like the first time he'd seen her. His fingers ached to remove it, to see the light shimmering down the waves like it did that afternoon.

He forced his boots across the floor and found himself removing his hat. "I see you made it in okay."

She nodded. "Claire came home soon after I arrived. I didn't have to wait outside long."

"Why didn't you just come on in? The door's never locked."

A frown wrinkled her forehead. "I couldn't do that."

"Why not?"

"She's got some manners," Claire said, slapping Derek's hand off the biscuits. "Unlike some people around here."

Hank gave them a granite stare, then turned back to Alex. "Claire get you settled in, then?"

"Oh, yes, I'm all unpacked."

Her soft drawling voice melted around him like the sun on a warm summer day. "We appreciate you cooking tonight, seeing as how you just got in."

"That's my job, isn't it?"

He nodded, then the hands began to complain about delaying supper. "We'll talk after we eat."

He placed a hand at the small of her back and walked her around to the empty chair at the end of the table nearest the kitchen. Releasing her reluctantly, he pulled out the chair.

Alex quickly sat. She murmured a brief thank you, then pulled her napkin out as Hank moved to his seat at the other end.

The hands reached for the nearest platters of food but stopped when he cleared his throat. "Let's say grace first, boys."

They looked at him as if he'd declared he was half Brahma bull. He stared each of them into removing their hats and bowing their heads. Alex and Claire smiled at him, then lowered their heads. Hank bowed his own head and tried to remember prayers his father had uttered. Failing that, he settled for a shorter, customized version of the prayer he'd heard at countless rodeos.

When he finished, Alex raised her head, smiling at the unique prayer. She opened her mouth to comment it, but instead her jaw fell slack.

The men attacked the food as if they hadn't been fed in a week. Forks and serving spoons blended with hands and arms as they vied to see who could fill his plate the fastest. They looked like a pack of dogs descending on one bowl of food.

Making no attempt to join the fray, Alex caught Claire's eye.

The girl leaned over. "I told you."

"Is it always this bad?"

Claire nodded. "Better get some food while the getting's good. There won't be a crumb left in five minutes."

Alex grabbed a biscuit as the plate passed, then settled back in her chair to watch the men consume their food with voracious appetites. Nobody said a single word until every scrap had disappeared down their gullets. The only male that had a modicum of manners was Hank. Though he didn't say anything, either, he didn't act like a lion about to devour a Christian.

When all was gone, they looked at her expectantly.

She chuckled. "Yes, I made dessert."

They yahooed as she went to get two warm cheese pies.

"Sure was tasty, Alex," Jed said as he rose from the table. "You even cooked the steaks right."

"Claire told me you like them just this side of charred."

"Well, we're mighty glad you're here."

Jed's words caught Alex off guard. How long had it been since someone cared whether she was around or not? But instead of making her happy, the warm, fuzzy feeling frightened her. She didn't belong with these people. This was just a temporary job. After she said goodbye four weeks from now, she'd probably never see them again.

She stood abruptly to gather the dinner plates. "Thanks, Jed."

The other hands added their compliments as they followed Jed out.

"You coming, boss?" Buck asked as he paused in the doorway.

Hank leaned back in his chair. "I'll be along directly. Get that new mare warmed up and the calves in the pen."

Alex had learned that the three hands worked on this ranch because of the time Hank spent with them on their roping and riding skills as they trained stock for the rodeo. Every night after supper, they turned on the floodlights illuminating the large corral and worked on roping calves or riding wild horses.

Claire told her Hank had a reputation on the rodeo circuit for the roping horses he trained. Derek had come all the way from Texas to work with Hank and learn from him.

Alex could feel Hank's gaze on her as she scraped the dinner dishes. She darted a glance at him. The heat in his eyes made her drop the stack of dishes she was moving from one place to the next too quickly. They clattered loudly in the quiet room.

The look on his face meant trouble. Big trouble. It made her feel like a kettle boiling on the stove—steamy hot, with insides that wouldn't keep still. It made her wonder what those unsmiling lips would feel like against hers.

*No!* she told herself sharply. She was not looking for a man—not even one as handsome as Tom Cruise, Brad Pitt and Mel Gibson all rolled into one. No one—not even a blue-eyed, square-jawed cowboy—was going to stop her from getting to San Francisco. She'd wasted half her life waiting for someone wonderful to walk in and give her a home, a connection. First at the orphanage, then at all the places she'd worked. She was through waiting. She had a plan and the determination to see it through.

To distract herself and him, she asked, "Did you enjoy supper?"

"Didn't you notice he had second helpings of everything?" Claire asked as she returned from carrying empty platters into the kitchen.

"I had three helpings of potatoes," Hank added. "So, yes, you could say I enjoyed supper."

Alex felt as if her bones were spreading across the floor as relief flooded through her. She didn't know until just then how important it had been to please him. Her hands halted for an instant as the realization sunk in. But wanting to please an employer was natural, wasn't it? She always wanted people to enjoy her cooking. Her livelihood depended on it.

She didn't want to listen to the inner voice reminding her that pleasing someone's palate had never left her weak in the knees, so she pushed it away and scraped harder.

"Might as well get our little chat over with now." Hank's deep voice resonated through the room.

"Okay, chat away," she said as she picked up another plate.

"Not here," he said firmly. "The tax papers are up in my office."

Alex's hands stopped in mid-scrape. The last thing she needed right now was to be alone with this man. Maybe later, when she wasn't so on edge, when the air between them didn't crackle with tension. "I need to clean up first."

He rose to his full six feet. "Claire can finish."

"But I should—"

"Go on, Alex," Claire urged. "I can do this."

Alex tore her eyes away to survey the table. Claire nearly had it cleared. Looked like there was no way to avoid this. Damn. She placed the plate she held on top of the stack, untied her apron and turned to Hank.

He swept his arm toward the door. "After you."

Claire had given Alex a tour of the house when they had supper well under way, so she knew the second floor of the ranch house consisted of three large bedrooms, plus a bathroom and the ranch office that had been carved from the fourth bedroom. As Alex climbed the straight flight of stairs past pictures of Edens dead and living, she was vividly aware that the man ascending behind her was so close she could feel the warmth of his hard, lean body. There was an intimacy in climbing the stairs together. Alex didn't want to think about the way their bodies moved in concert—right foot, left foot, right—but she couldn't help it.

She paused when she came up into the hallway that bisected the second floor. The layout of rooms echoed the four-square pattern of the first floor. To her left, the door to the office, which was directly over her bedroom, stood open. Claire referred to it as the sanctuary. Hank retreated there after training sessions every night, wrestling with the paperwork the ranch required.

Alex took a deep breath as Hank stepped up beside her. He placed his hand on the small of her back, and heat spread through her. Though he didn't push, he exerted enough pressure to urge her on.

"It's not a torture chamber."

Alex gave him a weak smile, then turned away as heat stung her cheeks. Why did she feel so apprehensive? Hank was just another boss in a long line of bosses. This was not the first time she'd sat with one alone in his or her office. But she couldn't push the feeling away.

Hank moved behind a desk cluttered with papers and magazines. A lamp stood at one end. As he reached to turn it on, dust fell from the shade. He didn't seem to notice. Behind the desk, a small table held a computer. Two chairs sat on this side of the desk, but both were stacked with magazines so she made no move to sit down. Two walls were covered with bookshelves crammed with books on everything from gardens to quilts to turn-of-the-century animal husbandry. As she scanned the titles, one of them twitched.

"Sugar! So this is where you ran off to hide." Strength surged back into Alex's muscles, and she reached behind a row of books on quarter horses to pull the cat from the shelf. Sugar was familiar. Comforting him in a new place was familiar. She touched her nose to his before she faced Hank. "I'm sorry. I hope he didn't disturb anything. It always takes a week or so for him to feel at home in a new place. But he won't spray or claw anything."

"He's okay."

She nodded and to keep from looking at him, she glanced around his desk. "You writing a novel or something? Sure are a lot of papers."

He shrugged. "Ranches aren't just cows and horses. I spend as much time on paperwork as I do on horseback—paying invoices, keeping up with correspondence, checking on beef prices, reading about farm legislation."

"You must work late at night, then."

"Sometimes. Why?"

"Well, my bed is right below your desk and I'm a light sleep—" She trailed off at the blazing look in his eyes. Why did she have to bring the word *bed* into the conversation?

Hank cleared his throat. "I'll try not to disturb you."

"Oh, don't worry about me. I'll be fine. You just do what you need to do. You're the boss, after all, and your work is very important. I'm just—" She stopped abruptly. "I'm babbling, aren't I?"

His lips twitched, but didn't quite form a smile. "Yep."

She took a deep breath. "Then I'll shut up."

"Why don't we sit down and get this over with?" he suggested.

She eyed the stack of *Western Horseman* magazines filling the chair.

Finally noticing the mess, Hank came around the desk and picked up the magazines. He looked around and for lack of a better place, plopped them on top of another stack of magazines on the corner table. A cloud of dust billowed up, but Hank ignored it like he always did.

"Sit," he commanded. He waited as she frowned down at the seat, then sat gingerly on the edge. While she settled the cat on her lap, he sank into his own chair and cleared his throat again. He noticed he was doing that a helluva lot around this woman. "The first thing I want to explain is that we don't stand on ceremony. Everybody's the same as everybody else. No exceptions. That clear?"

She nodded.

He stared down at his desk, then picked up a pencil. "Like I said, we need to get things clear on the front end."

She stared at the pencil his hands twirled. He shifted in his seat, wondering if she knew that he played with the pencil to keep his hands from doing what they really wanted to do.

She broke the silence with "Okay."

He glanced up, then down, then began to twirl the pencil again. "You're the cook. That's it in three words. We eat breakfast at sunrise and supper at six. We have lunch at noon if we're working around the place. If we're out on the range, we do without.''

"No.''

The pencil stopped twirling. "No? No what?''

"I mean, while I'm the cook, you won't do without lunch. You work hard and need your nourishment. I'll either pack you a lunch, or I'll bring it to you.''

Hank stared at her until she fidgeted in her seat. He'd never had a cook care whether he ate lunch or not. Even his mother never packed them a lunch. He realized his gaze was making her nervous when she amended her declaration.

"That is, if you don't mind.''

He pushed the pencil between his fingers, lead down, then eraser down. For some reason her suggestion touched him on a level so elemental that he felt warmth blossoming deep inside, but he didn't understand what it was or why. All he knew was an overwhelming urge to touch her. He had to clench his fingers around the pencil to keep them from reaching across the desk.

Hell, she surprised him, that's all. People usually avoided extra work. They didn't seek it out.

"Can you…'' He cursed inwardly when he had to clear the huskiness from his throat. "Can you ride?''

"Well, no, I've never been on a horse. Never had the opportunity. But I'm sure I can learn.''

He gave a brief nod, though his mind dwelled on the pleasurable prospect of teaching her. "I'll see that you do. I'm sure the boys would appreciate grub at noon. It's a mighty long time between meals otherwise. I've just never had a cook that I'd ask to make the trip.''

"Well, you didn't ask, did you?''

He felt one side of his mouth twitch. "No, ma'am, I didn't.'' When he realized she was squirming under his stare, he looked away.

"Anything else?'' she asked.

He drew a deep breath and tried to think. "Nope. That about covers it.''

She cleared her throat. The sound told him she felt the

charged atmosphere in the room as much as he did. That knowledge sent pricks of excitement over his already-raw nerves.

"If that's everything, I'll get out of your way," she said.

He stared at her so long and so hard that her eyes fell to the cat. He shook his head to clear away the image of the slender hands that massaged the orange fur. "That's it."

As she softly padded down the stairs, he realized he forgot to have her sign the tax forms. The pencil in his hands snapped.

Alex walked out onto the back porch and took a deep breath of the cool March air. She couldn't stand it. This was her third day at the Garden and if she didn't find something to do with all the hours between cleaning up the breakfast dishes and starting supper, she'd go absolutely bonkers. When she agreed to take the job she expected to spend the mornings fixing lunch, but because the men were working so far from the house she'd packed their lunch while they ate breakfast.

A meow at the screen door behind her brought her attention to Sugar, who rubbed against it.

"No, you're not used to the place, Sugar. If I let you out, you might run off and get lost. Then where would I be? I wouldn't even have a cat to talk to."

Alex sighed heavily, then wandered back into the house. She trailed her hand along a heavy linen chest, then tsked to find the tips of her fingers black.

"I can't believe they treat this beautiful old house so shabbily," she told Sugar, who rubbed against her leg. "Why, if I had a home like this, I'd keep it shining like a new penny. I'd—" She sighed deeply. "Why are you letting me talk like that? This isn't my home, and I don't care if the dust is waist-deep."

Alex wandered through the downstairs rooms, desperate to find something to occupy her time and determined to ignore the dirt. But the more she told herself she didn't care, the more the rooms called out to her. The heavy oak furniture in the dining room would be so beautiful if it just had a coat of wax.

The curtains in the living room were dingy with smoke, and the colors of the rug were muted by dirt.

Finally she could stand it no longer.

"Like Sister Mary Clara said," she told Sugar as she gathered cleaning supplies from the mud room. "Idle hands are the devil's workshop."

Three hours later, she flipped off the vacuum and stood back to survey her handiwork. Stripped of its dingy coat, the parlor looked like an entirely different room. It gleamed with soft highlights and smelled of wax and flowers.

"What's going on?"

Alex squealed and spun around to see Hank standing in the wide doorway. His hands were planted on his hips, and he glowered at her.

Feeling like she'd just been caught with her hand in the cookie jar, Alex pulled off the bandana tied around her hair. "I was just doing a little cleaning."

"That's Claire's job," he said harshly.

"Well, it doesn't look like she's doing it."

"No, it doesn't, and she's going to hear about it when she gets home."

"Look, I don't want to cause Claire trouble, I just want something to do."

"You're the cook, not the maid."

Alex threw her hands in the air. "Cooking takes up less than half the day, since I fix your lunch in the morning. I'm bored stiff the rest of the time."

"I'm sorry. But if you start doing Claire's chores around here, she's going to get as spoiled as a lady's mare. I don't ask her to do much, but I do expect her to keep up the house. She needs to learn responsibility."

Alex's eyes narrowed. "You're acting like you caught me rustling cattle or something. I'm just doing a little cleaning. It's not a felony."

A muscle in his jaw twitched. "Just stick to your cooking."

"Or what?" she demanded. "You'll fire me?"

Silence fell over the room. If she'd been combustible, she'd have gone up in flames from the heat in his eyes. She had him and his ridiculous demands over a barrel, and they both knew it. But she didn't feel any triumph.

"Look, I just need something to do. I'm bored here all d…" She trailed off as he walked slowly toward her. Ensnared by the intense, dangerous light in his eyes, Alex stood transfixed as he approached.

He didn't stop until he was just inches away. She could feel the heat his large body generated, smell the faint odor of horses and sweat, see the flat line of his full, unsmiling lips.

"You're the damnedest woman," he said softly. "I've never met one that would argue a blue streak about doing more work."

"I…I just need something to do besides cooking." Alex heard the breathlessness in her voice, but she couldn't help it. "And this old house needs somebody who…"

She trailed off again as his eyes dropped to her mouth. His thoughts were so clear she could read them as if they flashed across his forehead. He wanted to kiss her.

She forced her eyes away and stepped back, frightened, not because he wanted to kiss her but because she wanted him to.

She heard him cuss under his breath and he pulled the brim of his hat lower. "Oh, hell. At least make Claire help so we can still pretend it's her chore. It'll be her responsibility when you're gone, after all."

Alex nodded. "Okay."

He stood there so long that she glanced up to see him looking around the room. His face softened as his eyes made the circuit. "I haven't seen it look this good since Momma died. Momma loved this old house. She kept it shining from floor to ceiling."

Alex felt her heart squeeze painfully. She didn't know the full story, just that Hank's parents died suddenly. "How did she die, if you don't mind me asking?"

Pain flashed across his face. "In a flash flood. My father, too."

Alex wanted to reach out to him. She knew how much losing one parent hurt. To lose two at the same time… "That's when you left the rodeo, isn't it? You came home so your parents' and grandparents' dream wouldn't die.''

He looked at her as if he didn't know what she meant. "I came home to take care of Travis and Claire. That was eight years ago.''

"Eight years? That means Claire was only nine when your mother died. Maybe she neglects her chores because she's never been shown how to do them. I mean, she doesn't have a mother to show her how, and if your cooks didn't do house-work, how can you expect Claire to know how?''

He shrugged. ''It's women's work.''

It took an effort, but she managed not to roll her eyes. "Women aren't born knowing how to clean a toilet, Mr. Eden. We have to learn how to do housework just like you had to learn to rope a cow—by example and practice.''

He regarded her for the space of three breaths. ''Hank,'' he said.

"What?''

"I'm just Hank, not Mr. Eden. Like I told you the day you arrived, we don't stand on ceremony around here.''

"All right...Hank. So it's okay if I spend my extra time cleaning up the house? I promise I'll make Claire help.''

He shrugged.

"Good. So, was there something in particular you wanted? You're not usually home in the middle of the day. Checking up on me?''

"No, I was close by the house and remembered I had to—'' Hank frowned, unable to remember why he'd come home. He had a legitimate reason. What was it? Oh, yeah. ''To make a phone call about some serum I've been expecting.''

"Oh, that reminds me.'' She wiped her hands on her apron and turned. ''You got a call this morning.''

Grateful for a crack in the tension, Hank followed her into the kitchen and took the note she handed him. He saw that it was the name and number of the real estate agent that was handling the sale of the ranch.

"Is it about your serum?'' she asked.

Hank shook his head. "But I need to return this call, too. I'm glad I stopped by."

"I won't keep you, then."

He nodded briskly, turned on his heel and climbed the stairs. Entering his office, he closed the door firmly and sat down behind his desk. He stared blindly at the dust on the lampshade for a long moment.

What the hell was wrong with him? All Alex had been doing was cleaning, for God's sake. What kind of provocation was that? But the way his body reacted, she might as well have been doing a table dance. Never had he been aroused so much by so little.

This was insane. He had to get that woman off his mind, and keep her off. To that end, he took several deep breaths, then reached for the phone. He called about the serum first. It was in. He'd send Casey to fetch it tomorrow. His foreman's wife, Lila, would probably enjoy the trip into town.

Then he dialed the real estate agent.

"Ranch Realty, Cheyenne Office," said a cheerful female voice.

"Dennis Cowden, please."

"One moment."

After a few seconds of elevator music, a friendly tenor voice said, "Dennis Cowden."

"Mr. Cowden, this is Hank Eden in Dubois. I got the message you called this morning."

"Mr. Eden, glad you called. I got a fax this morning with our first offer."

He named an amount that made Hank lean back in his chair.

"Course we're not gonna take it."

Hank sat up. "Why the hell not? That's more than you thought we'd—"

"That's right. But hell, it's only been a month. Let's give the big boys time to get in on the action. Corporations take a little longer to come up with an offer, you understand. So many people have to approve things. But I think we'll see a substantial improvement over this offer." The agent sounded enormously pleased with himself. "Yes, indeedy I do."

"All right, then. I reckon you know what you're doing."

Hank hung up the phone thoughtfully. Damn, that was a lot of money. Claire and Travis were going to be poleaxed when he told them what their share of the sale would be. Should he go ahead and tell them about the sale?

No. He'd better wait until they got the best offer. No sense worrying them over details.

Hank turned and stared out the window at the barn he knew like the back of his hand. In a few months he'd be out from under the burden of running this place, and back on the rodeo circuit with a hell of a lot of change in his pocket. He should be jumping up and down with joy.

Why wasn't he?

# Chapter Three

As she filled the coffeepot with water, Alex saw the hands heading to the house for supper. She set the pot down, grabbed a large meat fork and ran to cut them off at the pass. Stationing herself in the mud room, she stood with legs spread and arms akimbo.

Jed entered first, laughing at some joke they'd just shared. He stopped when he saw her, but was nudged in by Derek's forward motion.

Buck craned to see around Derek. "Hey! What's plugging up the chute?"

"We got us a little filly up here, looks like she's riled up and ready to buck," Jed said over his shoulder.

"Howdy, Alex," Derek said placatingly. "Something sure smells good."

Aware of Claire coming up behind her, Alex waved her fork at them. "You're not having any supper until you take off your boots and hats."

"What'd she say?" Buck called from behind.

"She wants us to take off our boots and hats," Derek told him.

"Don't she know cowboys don't take off their hats for nothing 'cept prayer and sleepin'?"

"I reckon not."

"Tell her."

"Ma'am, you must have rocks in your head if you think we're gonna—"

"You want any supper?"

With the fork waving under his nose, Jed leaned back into the men pushing him forward. "Yes'm, we do."

"Then take them off." Alex knew stubbornness was all she had on her side. Since the shortest one probably outweighed her by fifty pounds, they could easily push her aside and walk on in. "This is a mud room. It was built for muddy boots. And those shelves aren't decoration. They are there to put your—"

"What's going on?" Hank's deep voice floated through the door.

Grinning at her as if certain he'd back them up, the hands stepped aside to let the boss through.

"She's demanding that we take off our boots and hats, just for supper!" Jed complained.

Hank stepped into the mud room. Alex's golden-brown eyes were blazing and her chin rose a notch as he came in. With an apron around her trim waist and a small pitchfork in her hand, she reminded him of his mother. He'd seen Sarah Eden face down an even bigger bunch of cowpokes, and win. Though taller and slimmer than his mother, Alex had the same grit.

"I'm not asking much," Alex said. "But I spent all day putting a shine on that floor and—"

His eyes narrowed. "*You* spent all day?"

Her eyes cut back to Claire. "I mean, *we* spent the afternoon—"

"Did you help with that floor?" Hank asked his sister.

"I helped put down the wax when I got home," she told him defensively. "Alex had already stripped the old stuff off."

Hank tried to wither Alex with a look, but instead her chin set. "It doesn't matter who did the work. I want to keep it clean. Your men haven't been treating this house like it's your home, they treat it like a barn. And so do you.''

Hank's eyes narrowed, but instead of giving her a lesson in who was boss, he stepped into the hall. The only light illuminating the long expanse came from the dining room, but in its light he could see a faint sheen that he hadn't seen in many years. The pungent, clean smell of wax assailed his senses. He hadn't known he associated that smell with his mother until this very minute.

Guilt hit him as he realized how much the house had suffered during the past eight years. His mother had loved this house and kept it shining inside and out. Seeing it on a daily basis, he hadn't realized it was slowly deteriorating. He saw it now as Alex must see it. Everything in it was dull and caked with dirt—the floors, the curtains, the furniture.

Hank's eyes rested on his sister, but he couldn't really blame her. He'd thrown the housework at Claire when their second cook left, thinking she could cope with it at age eleven.

The heavy weight of responsibility he'd carried for eight years descended again. It had been weighing him down since his parents died and left him a ranch deep in debt and two young siblings to raise. Every time he thought he'd lifted that weight—when he'd begun recording ranch operations with black ink instead of red; when Travis left to make his fortune on the rodeo circuit; when he realized Claire was finally grown—it descended again. Each time it came down heavier than before. Each time it made him chafe at the bit a little harder.

He hadn't asked for this responsibility. He'd been a happy-go-lucky cowboy riding rough stock in every rodeo he could. He'd reveled in the hard life of a rodeo cowboy. He liked the hard bed of the camper on the back of his truck. He drank hard and loved every woman he could get his hands on. He knew he would inherit the Garden one day, but he always thought that day wouldn't come until he'd grown too old for the circuit and settled down on the ranch with one of the curvaceous buckle bunnies he met along the way. He'd expected to raise his own children, not his brother and sister. He'd expected the ranch to feel like security, not a millstone.

Hank met Alex's questioning eyes. This little lady had been at the Garden all of five days and already she was turning his life upside-down and inside-out. If he wasn't pondering the way her jeans clung to her round hips instead of taking care of the ranch paperwork, he was dusting off his pants before he sat down on a chair.

Trouble was, Alex was absolutely right. He hadn't treated this house like a home, because it didn't feel like *his* home. It still felt like his father's. To Hank, the Garden had been a place to hang his hat until time for him to leave. He hadn't cared whether he came home at night or camped out with the cattle—until the past five days.

Muttering a curse under his breath, Hank turned away from her expectant face. Giving a damn was the last thing he needed. Giving a damn meant he was getting soft. He had plans, and he didn't want anything to get in his way—not even a pair of angel eyes attached to a body made for sin. He didn't need to be reminded of how much the house meant to his mother. Not now. It was too late. The wheels to sell the ranch were already in motion. He wasn't about to put on the brakes. He didn't even want to.

Realizing he was taking a long time to make a decision, Hank threw a hard glance at his men. Hell, a clean house might help sell the ranch, so what harm would it do to give in?

He took off his hat and placed it on a shelf. When he sat on the bench and put his right heel in the boot jack, the hands grumbled, but took off their hats and waited their turn at the jack.

"That's not fair!"

Claire's words screamed down the stairs as Alex wiped off the stove. Startled by the harsh sound, she took half a step toward the open door between the kitchen and dining room. Hank's reply stopped her. His voice was lower, but held an edge of steel unmistakable to her, one floor below.

"Life isn't fair. Get used to it."

"Mallory's parents are letting her go! Why can't I? Give me one good reason."

"I don't care what Mallory's parents let her do. You're not going there with just Mallory as chaperone. What's wrong with Riverton? Or Lander?"

"We've already looked in all the stores in those one-horse towns. I hate being stuck in the rear end of nowhere!"

"Don't use language like that."

Realizing she was eavesdropping, Alex shook herself and closed the swinging door. It didn't help because their voices escalated.

"You're not my father! Why do you get to tell me what to do?"

"I'm your guardian, that's why. Until you turn eighteen on May eighth, I'm responsible for you."

"Mom and Dad must've been crazy to make you our guardian! You're nothing but a mean old man who's forgotten how to have fun."

There was a slight pause before Hank's low, tight voice said, "You don't know what *mean* is. If Dad were still alive, he'd—"

"He'd what?"

"Never mind."

"This is all your fault, anyway! I didn't even want to go to the stupid prom. You forced me to accept the invitation from Ty Jordan. All I'm trying to do is find a stupid dress to wear to the stupid prom! And you won't even let me do that!"

Hank's voice came down a notch, so Alex had to strain to hear.

"If you don't go to your senior prom, you'll regret it. Surely there's a dress here in Dubois that will fit you. If not here, then Riverton or Lander."

"Haven't you heard a single word I've said? There aren't any suitable dresses anyplace I've been. That's why I want to go to Laramie with Mallory. The university is there, and they are bound to have decent dresses with all the parties that go on."

"I'm sorry, Claire."

"I can't believe this! I'll be living in Laramie next year when I start college."

"That's next year. You're not going to Laramie alone with Mallory. That's final. Now get downstairs and help with the dishes. Alex does all your work around the house, so it's the least you can do."

The slam of a door reverberated through the house, startling Alex back into action. She felt color rise to her cheeks as she realized she'd been eavesdropping like a common snoop.

As she began loading glasses into the dishwasher, she heard Claire's angry footsteps descending the stairs. A minute later the teenager shoved the swinging door so hard it rammed the counter.

"I hate him!" she cried.

"No, you don't," Alex said softly. "He's your brother."

"You heard?"

She shrugged. "You were so loud I couldn't help it."

Claire threw her hands in the air as she paced from the stove to the door of the walk-in freezer. "Can you believe how mean he is? I'm almost eighteen! I'm old enough to go a few miles down the road by myself."

"Laramie is three hundred miles away. That qualifies for more than just a few. That's a good day's drive."

"It's less than four hours," Claire exclaimed.

"Not if you're going the speed limit."

"All right, five hours, then. What's the big deal?"

"That's ten hours going and coming. When were you going to shop?"

"If we left at five, we'd get there before noon. We could shop until six and still be home by midnight. We had it all planned, but Hank has to ruin it."

Alex shook her head. "I'm afraid I agree with Hank. You're far too young to be—"

"You're only eight years older than I am," Claire pointed out. "And you came all the way from Alabama by yourself."

Alex's chin rose at the reminder of the differences between

them. "That's different. I didn't have anyone at home worrying about me."

Claire's face softened and she gave Alex a hug. "Well, you do now. I wish you didn't have to leave. I know you've only been here a few days, but I feel like you're my sister."

The words touched Alex deeply. "Thanks. But I didn't mean to get sappy. I was just wondering…"

"What?" Claire prompted when she didn't continue.

"My day off is Saturday, right?"

"Well, I thought so. I mean, that's when all the other housekeepers' days off were, but you cooked last Saturday, so I—"

"I'd only been here two days then," Alex explained. "It didn't seem right to take a day off when I'd only worked one full day. But that doesn't matter. Are you and Mallory planning to go to Laramie on Saturday?"

"Yes, this Saturday."

"Do you think Hank might let you go if I went along to chaperone?"

Claire's face lit up as if someone plugged in a Christmas tree. "Would you?"

"Sure, I don't mind. It might be fun."

Claire gave her an exuberant hug. "Thank you!"

"This dress must mean a lot to you."

"Dress? Heck, no. Mallory's the one who's hot to go there for a dress. I want to see the campus of the university. I haven't seen it in several years and since I'll be going there this fall, I want to look around."

"Why didn't you tell your brother that?"

Claire wrinkled her nose in disgust. "He wouldn't let me go just for that."

"Well, he still might not. Better go ask if that will suit him."

"Okay!" Claire gave her another hug, then turned to leave. She stopped in her tracks. "Oh, the kitchen. I'm supposed to—"

"Go on," Alex urged. "It'll just take a minute to ask. There'll still be plenty of dirty pots and pans left when you get back."

Claire threw her a look of such thankfulness and joy that Alex felt her heart twist into a knot. She watched blindly as the door settled back on its hinges in decreasing swings.

Had she ever been that young and carefree?

Several hours later, Alex wiped her hands on the frayed dish towel and scanned the kitchen one last time. Supper dishes and pans were clean and stored. Breakfast and the next day's lunch were as far along as she could take them before sunrise.

Content with the progress, she checked on Sugar. The cat ran free in the house during the day, but as the sun began to disappear, Alex put him in her room so he wouldn't be stomped underfoot.

Feeling restless, Alex left Sugar to his nightly cleaning ritual and wandered onto the back porch. The temperature had fallen with the sun, but instead of retreating back inside, she meandered over to the swing hanging at one end and lowered herself into it. The thermometer would dip close to freezing by morning.

Recalling Claire's warm words earlier warmed Alex even as it made her sad. Sister. How she'd longed for one when she was growing up. But she'd heard declarations like Claire's from friends before, and when hard times came, those statements proved to be worth nothing more than the air they were carried on. Since she'd be moving on in three weeks, Claire's would no doubt prove as worthless. Still, it felt good to hear the words.

From her swinging perch, she surveyed the part of the sky she could see. So many stars. Which was her lucky one? If she knew, she would wish on it every night for…for what? She had what she wanted, didn't she? The chance to study under a master chef.

"Howdy, Alex. What's up?"

Derek's deep voice startled her out of her thoughts. "Nothing's changed since supper. You here to get more of that chocolate pie?"

"Well, now, if you're wanting to get rid of it, I'd be willing to force it down my throat, but…"

"Yes?" Alex prompted, though she knew what was coming.

"Is Miss Claire anywheres about?"

Alex was glad it was dark so he couldn't see the pity in her eyes. Derek came up to the house every night, asking after Claire. He'd fallen in love with the girl, that much was obvious. But his love was unrequited. The first night Alex went upstairs to tell Claire she had a gentleman caller, Claire made it very clear that she had no interest in Derek or any other cowboy. Claire considered cowboys filthy, unkempt fellows who wouldn't know romance if it came up and grabbed their horse by the tail. She planned to get her degree and find a good job in a big city like Chicago, Dallas or Denver.

"Claire's studying, Derek. I think she's got a calculus test tomorrow."

Derek nodded and pushed his hat back on his head. In the light coming through the screen door, he made a sad attempt at a grin. "Well, you can't blame a fella for trying."

"I'll get you that pie."

A few minutes later they were back on the porch. Alex set the swing moving again while Derek sat on the top step and fed on the chocolate dessert. A few minutes later Jed and Buck wandered up, and Alex got up to cut them each a piece of pie.

As they ate, Alex asked them questions about the ranch and their jobs. They talked freely, and eventually the conversation turned to Alex and why she didn't ride.

"You mean you ain't never sat on a horse?" Jed exclaimed. "There's gotta be a law!"

"I've never had the opportunity. There weren't any horses at…where I grew up." She hadn't told anyone about her days at the orphanage and didn't intend to.

"Hell, we'll teach ya," Buck said. "'Tween the three of us, we could learn anybody how to ride."

"That's my job."

They all turned to see Hank's silhouette in the doorway.

The screen door squeaked as he pushed it open. "I told her I'd teach her, I just haven't had time."

"Sure, boss," Derek said.

The hands shared a smiling look as Hank walked over to Alex. "May I join you?"

She stopped the swing and scooted to the far left. His descending weight made the chains rattle, then one boot set the swing back in motion.

Alex swallowed hard as his nearness sent her senses reeling. He smelled clean, like the soap in the upstairs bathroom. But underneath he emanated an odor that was heavier, muskier. It made her want to lean toward him and take a deep breath. His heat also acted like a magnet. She had to hang on to the arm of the swing to keep from moving toward him. With her right side heating up and her left side in the cold, she couldn't control the shiver that skimmed along her spine.

Hank interrupted his discussion with the hands about which horse would make her a good mount. "You cold?"

Alex ran her hand up her left arm. "A little. I'm okay."

Without another word, he rose and stepped inside. A few seconds later he returned carrying the lined denim jacket she'd seen on him nearly every day.

"Lean forward," he commanded.

She leaned, and he swung the jacket around her shoulders, then settled back on the swing. The conversation took up where he'd left it, but Alex barely noticed. That musky male odor she'd noticed earlier rose to her nostrils in powerful waves, mingled with the scents of horses, hay and fresh air.

Such a small kindness, so casually extended. It probably meant nothing to him. But it meant the world to someone who'd never belonged anywhere. Sure, most people were nice to her, but they never went out of their way to make her comfortable. They didn't care enough one way or another.

Until now.

"That all right with you? Hey, you awake?"

Alex's eyes flew open when Hank's hand touched her knee. Warm and heavy, it settled there, sending sparks shooting up her leg. "What?"

"We're going to put you on Maisy. She's gentle enough for a beginner. I'll try to make it in early tomorrow afternoon to give you your first lesson. Okay?"

"Sure." Alex cleared the frog suddenly caught in her throat. "Whatever you say. Don't go to any trouble just for—"

Hank squeezed her knee. "Hell, woman, it's not for you. We've got to get you riding if we're gonna have any grub at all on the drive."

Alex glanced down at the broad hand resting easily on her leg. How could simple pressure cause such havoc all over her body? Her blood felt like stampeding horses, racing through her veins with pounding hooves.

She shivered from more than the cold. There was no mistaking this as a friendly gesture. This was a man-woman gesture—a possessive man-woman gesture. Even so, her first instinct was to cover his hand with her own. The warm weight on her leg felt familiar, felt right. It made her feel things she had no business feeling—like maybe this man cared for her, like she belonged.

"Alex? You'll be here for the drive, won't you?"

Derek's question snapped her mind back to reality. She crossed her legs, and Hank removed his hand. "When is it?"

"In two weeks," Hank said.

"Then I'll still be here." Her heart still racing, she turned to Hank, only able to look at him because it was dark. "I'll be glad to learn to ride whenever someone has time to teach me."

"I'll be teaching you, and we'll shoot for tomorrow, if that's okay. For now, I think it's time some cowpokes turned in. Sunrise comes mighty early."

Alex rose as the hands grumbled good-naturedly and wandered toward the bunk house. She removed Hank's jacket, and he opened the door for her.

"Thanks for the loan." She handed Hank his coat without meeting his eyes.

"No problem." He took the coat and draped it over the hook beneath his hat. He turned but made no move to leave. The air between them felt electric.

Uncomfortable with his eyes on her, Alex cast around in her mind for a safe subject. Relief flooded through her as she remembered one. "Would you like a piece of pie?"

"Is there any left?"

Sure of herself now that she could feed somebody, she moved into the kitchen straight to the refrigerator.

Hank walked in behind her.

"I saved it for you. I've heard you moving around in here late at night—" She froze with her grip on the door handle as she realized what she'd said. To cover what might be considered an innuendo—it sure felt like one to her—she opened the refrigerator, pulled out a plate and set it on the table. "Anyway, I found things missing the next morning, so I know you've been getting hungry. The hands have been eating up all the dessert. Tonight I thought I'd cut you a piece first, before they got to it. I mean, you're the boss and all. You should have first crack at it."

Every muscle in Hank's body grew hard as he stared down at the extralarge piece of chocolate pie while she went to get a fork. Every time he thought he'd gotten past this stupid attraction that neither of them wanted, she went and did something like this.

It wasn't much, just a piece of pie. But it meant she thought about him, just like he thought about her. If only she knew what drove him downstairs in the middle of the night, she'd probably run screaming to her little yellow car and take off like a mare chased by a grizzly. It was hunger, all right, but not the kind she meant, though he ended up trying to appease it with mere food. Knowing that she'd heard him, that she lay awake while he stared at her closed door, sent heat shattering through him.

"Coffee?"

Hank hoped the intensity in his body didn't show in his face as he met her eyes. "Sure." He had to force his muscles to relax before he could bend enough to settle in the chair. As he sat, she set the coffee cup next to his plate. He found it strong and black, just the way he liked it.

He picked up the fork and dug into the pie. She sat quietly across from him, sipping a glass of ice water. He ate steadily, trying not to dwell on how her eyes followed every trip of the fork from the plate to his mouth.

He finally set the fork across the plate, took a sip of coffee and cleared his throat. "About this trip to Laramie…"

She sat up. "Is it okay? I don't want to usurp your authority, but it seemed to mean a lot to Claire, and I wanted to help."

"You don't have to give up your day off to chaperone a couple of silly girls on a shopping trip. They can make do with—"

"I don't mind. Really. I mean, I don't have anything else to do. Unless you'd rather they didn't go at all."

Hank shook his head. "I'm not a monster, no matter what she says. I just don't think it's a good idea to set a couple of girls loose in a rough cow town like Laramie. If you'll go with them, I'm happy. When she came back upstairs, I was trying to figure out how I could get my chores done so I could take them."

Alex cocked her head. "Does Claire know that?"

"No."

"Don't you think it'd help if you told her?"

He frowned. "Why would it?"

She looked down, then back at him, then away again.

"Go ahead and say it before you bust a gut," he said.

She sighed. "What the heck, all you can do is fire me. Then you'd be out the money you paid for my radiator. Mind if I give you a little friendly advice?"

"How friendly you talking about?"

"I've noticed that you're not too good at telling people the why of things. You just give an order and expect it to be obeyed."

His eyes narrowed. "I'm the boss."

"Of Claire?"

"I'm her legal guardian for another couple of months. I don't think I've done such a bad job raising her and Travis."

"No, you haven't. She's a beautiful young lady. It's just that she's about grown up. If you would explain things to her, let her know what's going on, she'd understand why you're making her do the things you do, or not letting her do the things she can't. Open up a little. You'd probably be surprised at how much closer you'll be." She smiled wryly. "It'd work with the hands, too, you know. I'm sure you have good reasons for the orders you give. If you told them why they're cleaning the tack for the second time that day, they probably wouldn't grumble so much."

He leaned back in his chair, as if he could get away from her words. Alex had just described his father. John Eden had never explained anything. Never told the crew why they had to work through lunch. Never told his sons he was proud of them, or that he loved them.

If Hank could dive into his gene pool and zap the genes he'd gotten from his father, he would. Hank had sworn years ago that he'd never walk in John Eden's boots. He would've punched any cowpoke that claimed he did.

Hank looked down at the arm he'd placed alongside his plate and saw that his hand was only inches from Alex's. Funny, he didn't feel like punching her. His fingers ached to stretch out and touch her helping hand. For the first time in eight years he had someone to help him, especially with Claire. Oh, the other cooks helped some, but only because they'd been paid to. None would've considered giving up their day off for a twelve-hour drive with two giggling teenagers. He felt a tiny bit of the weight on his shoulders lift, and the heat that had centered in one part of his anatomy spread throughout his body, warming even the marrow of his bones.

"I'm sorry if I spoke out of turn," she said into the silence. "And if the thought of talking to Claire is that hard, I'll tell her that you were planning to—"

"No, it's not that. It's…too complicated to go into." Damn, he was clamming up again—just like his father. He drew breath to explain further and was relieved when Alex spoke first.

"If all this was so much trouble, why did you insist Claire go to the prom?"

Hank straightened in his chair. "If she doesn't go, she'll regret it one day. It's a part of growing up, and she needs to experience it. Hell, she's not involved in anything at school. She can at least do this."

"Didn't you go to your senior prom?"

Surprised, he met her eyes squarely. She had a way of seeing straight to the heart of the matter that disturbed him, but at the same time made him hot. "No."

"Why not? With your good looks, I'm sure you could've found a date."

He paused for the space of two ragged breaths. "You think I'm good-looking?"

Her face went white and she looked down at her glass. "I didn't mean— Well, you—" Her wide eyes shot back up to his. "You know you are."

"I do?"

"Hank!"

The corners of his mouth curved upward.

Her mouth fell open.

"What?" he demanded.

"Do that again."

"Do what?"

"Smile."

He couldn't keep his mouth from obeying. That it almost hurt told him how long it had been since those muscles had made the effort. That it was this woman who made him feel like smiling worried him enough that it faded.

"You should do that more often," she said breathlessly.

He scowled. "I smile."

"Not so anyone would notice," she insisted. "But you still haven't answered my question."

"What question?"

"Why didn't you go to your senior prom?"

He tore his gaze away from hers. "I didn't go because I didn't have a senior year in high school."

"You didn't graduate?"

"I took the GED in March of my junior year so I could cut out."

"Cut out of what?"

"Hell, home. The ranch. What else?"

"Why?"

He shoved the chair back with a loud scrape, about to get

up. He'd never told anyone how he felt about his father. He didn't know if he could start now.

But Hank didn't rise. For some reason he couldn't fathom, he wanted to tell Alex. And it wasn't just to prove he wasn't like his father. Was it to see how she'd react? To make her take off in her little yellow car so this damned attraction would go away? Or did he want to see if she could ease this burden for him, too? She said it helped to open up. Maybe the reason he hadn't was that he'd never had anyone who cared enough to listen.

"My father," he said more harshly than he intended. He cleared his throat and started again. "Claire—and Travis, too—believe Dad was such a great guy, but they didn't know him like I did. They think I'm hard." He released a bitter laugh. "I'm a feather pillow compared to him. He was after me constantly, pushing me, working me. Nothing I ever did was good enough. The argument between Claire and me earlier was nothing compared to the rows I used to have with Dad."

"So you left home when you were...what? Seventeen?"

He nodded and finally met her eyes. The tenderness and sympathy there made some nameless something—some black, twisted knot deep inside him begin to unravel. "Barely."

"What did you do?"

"Rodeo. It's what I'd been doing for ten years to get away on the weekends. It became my life until they died."

"You were pretty good at it, weren't you?"

"I was on my way to the National Finals." His brows suddenly came together. "Why the sad look?"

"Sorry." Alex took a deep breath to supply her lungs with air. Why else would her apology sound as breathless as it did?

He must've heard in it more than she intended because his face softened and his voice lowered. "For me?"

She could feel her face flame and she looked down, but said bravely, "Yes, for you. I don't even remember my father, but at least my mother made me feel loved and wanted until she died."

"When did she die?"

Alex shook her head. "One soul-baring is quite enough for one evening, don't you think?"

Hank bristled. He'd obviously taken her offer to open up too seriously. "I've never told anybody how I felt about my father. I shouldn't have—"

"Don't be sorry," she said, covering his hand with hers.

He stared down at her hand so long that she began drawing it away. He immediately caught her fingers and brought them to his lips. The warmth of his mouth raced from her hand along every nerve in her body, leaving her breathless and weak with longing.

"Thanks for listening," he said.

Their eyes met over their joined hands and held. Alex didn't know how long the spell lasted. It could've been an eternity or just a few short seconds before the grandfather clock in the hallway chimed ten times.

Alex pulled her hand away. "Five o'clock comes awful early."

He nodded, and they both stood. An awkward moment passed in silence, then they spoke at the same time.

"Look, I—"

"I've been—"

Alex smiled and Hank's mouth twitched in reply. She felt as if her stomach were free floating inside her body.

"You first," he insisted.

"No, you go ahead."

"Alex…"

"Okay." She took a deep breath. "I just need…I mean I don't want to be a bother, but—"

"But what?" he pressed.

"It's just that I'm almost out of flour. And there's a few other things I could use if you want the good meals to continue."

He shook his head. "You were afraid to point out that we need supplies?"

"I just don't want to be any trouble. I mean, I'm only here for a few weeks and…" She trailed off at the look in his blue eyes.

"If that don't beat all," he said.

"What?"

"I've never met a woman who's ashamed of asking for necessities. Hell, you're cooking to fill our bellies."

"I'm not going to be here very long. I don't want to fill the pantry with things the next cook won't use."

Hank's eyes seemed to burn into hers. He took half a step toward her, then stopped himself. She could almost feel his muscles tense as he controlled whatever urge drove him.

The strong reaction took her by surprise. She stepped back and cleared her throat. "But flour is absolutely necessary."

The blue eyes holding hers took a moment to clear. When they finally did, he tore them away.

"You may not need much, but we do," he growled. "We'll go into town on Thursday, if that suits you."

"Sure, I—"

"Good night."

Alex stared after him as he strode from the room. First cold, then hot, then cold again. Would she ever understand this man?

Did she really want to?

# Chapter Four

As Alex pushed a pot roast into the oven to slow-cook, she heard the unmistakable sound of a horse's hooves clomping around outside the house. Two steps took her to the window over the sink in time to see Hank ride up to the barn.

She glanced at the clock and frowned. Three o'clock. Why was he home? Only once in the eight days she'd worked at the ranch had he ever made it home before the hands.

Hank stumbled as he dismounted, catching himself on the saddle.

Alex slammed the oven door closed and tossed her padded mittens on the counter as she ran out the door. She'd sprinted halfway across the yard before the screen door rattled against the jamb. She didn't slow until she reached the deep shadows of the barn. Her eyes hadn't even begun to adjust when a pair of strong arms caught her.

"What's wrong?" a deep familiar voice demanded.

"Hank?"

"What is it? What's wrong?"

"Are you okay?"

"Of course I'm okay. Are you?"

She could see him clearly now. His obvious concern made

her already-racing heart perform a backward flip in her chest. "I thought you might be...I mean, you almost fell when you dismounted."

His face softened, but his hold on her didn't relax. "I haven't been out of the saddle all day. My old knee injury was a little stiff, and it buckled on me."

She nodded, but her sigh of relief caught in her throat as his eyes seemed to ignite. She suddenly became aware of how close they stood. His strong fingers gripped her arms just above the elbows, pulling her against his muscled body. She could feel his warm breath flowing over her face like an intoxicating vapor. When he smiled, she thought she would faint from the brilliance of his white teeth against his sun-darkened face.

"We had a date, remember? I came to give you a riding lesson."

As his words sank in, Alex tried to will the color from creeping up her neck. She felt like a fool for jumping to conclusions, but more than that, she knew running out here in a panic made it look like she cared a little too much about what happened to him. Swallowing hard as she realized she did care, she lowered her gaze.

"What's wrong now?" he demanded, holding on.

She pulled back as far as he'd let her. "It's not a date."

His grip tightened as he drew a ragged breath, then he released her suddenly. "You're right, it's not. God forbid either of us forgets we have responsibilities."

She frowned. "I'm sorry. It's just that—"

"Yeah, I know. You're not sticking around. You made it perfectly clear when I hired you." He lifted the saddle from the gelding he'd ridden and threw it on the rack nailed into the wall. "Well, don't worry, little lady. I don't need romantic complications any more than you do. Thanks for the reminder."

Alex felt shards of disappointment stab through her. She took half a step toward him, but forced herself to stop. "Maybe it would be better if Jed or Buck taught me to ride."

"No!" He whirled from Maisy's stall door to glare at her.

"I'm the boss around here. I'll teach you. No one else. That clear?"

His hot words made Alex take a step back. They stared at each other across the expanse of the barn. Maisy blew at Hank from her stall. The blue heeler dogs barked at one another as they played in the meadow beyond. But these sounds barely registered in Alex's brain. All she could hear was Hank's harsh, uneven breathing. All she could see was his hard, implacable face. All she could feel was the magnetic force between them.

No! She wasn't attracted to this man. It was just the excitement of learning how to ride. But even as she tried to convince herself, she knew it wasn't true. Something about this cowboy drew her like nectar drew hummingbirds. How simple it would be to walk into his arms and taste that nectar. She knew without a doubt it would be incredibly sweet—so sweet she might never want to leave.

Alex dragged her eyes from his. Now the simple pleasure of learning to ride had been ruined. Instead of concentrating on the horse, she wouldn't be able to think of anything but those blue eyes watching her.

"Is what I have on okay?" She dug her fingernails into her palms, trying not to squirm as he looked her over slowly, insolently, from head to toe.

Finally he said, "You got better shoes than that? Something with heels and harder soles?"

She glanced down at her faux leather sport shoes. "I've got a pair of short heels for dresses, but—"

"Not those kinds of heels. Look." He lifted his foot. The deep brown leather boot was dull with dust, but the solid, stacked two-inch heels and the well-creased rounded toes looked much sturdier than anything she owned.

Alex shook her head. "This is the best I've got."

He shrugged. "They'll do for now. Thought we'd ride about an hour. That going to put a hardship on you fixing supper?"

Like he cared. "I've got a roast in the oven. It should be fine for a couple of hours, but I ran out here so fast I...I just need to check it first."

He nodded and turned away. "Fine. Be back in ten minutes."

"Yes, sir," she mumbled, and stalked toward the house. The instant she entered, the comforting smells and sounds surrounded her, soothing her. Her heart slowed to a normal pace as she made sure she hadn't unseated the lid on the pot when she'd slammed the oven door. The roast was fine and would be okay for another couple of hours.

Now all she had to do was put a lid on the hormones boiling inside her. This ranch and the people on it were far too tempting as it was. Not a day went by that Claire or Buck or someone didn't ask her to stay. If she succumbed to this attraction to Hank, she'd be lost. She might never make it to San Francisco.

Alex closed her eyes as her fingernails dug into her palms. Romances came and went, but what she would learn under Monsieur Buchaude would last the rest of her life. All she had to do was keep her perspective—and hope Hank kept his hands to himself.

As the screen door slammed, Hank spun around. His heel sprayed a shower of dirt across Maisy's stall door. He would've kicked the door if he didn't have to put a beginner on the mare before she'd have time to calm down.

What the hell was wrong with him? Coming on to Alex was just plain stupid, like a jackrabbit playing with a rattlesnake.

But when her wide, golden eyes turned on him, eating him up like candy, his thinking apparatus went on vacation. Those eyes.

For one brief second they saw nothing but him. They held concern. Almost like she cared about him, like she wanted him as much as he wanted her. That's the way it seemed…for one brief second.

Then his mouth opened without being connected to his brain, and she skittered away, like she was the jackrabbit and he the rattlesnake.

Hank leaned against the barn wall and threw his head back with a thump. She was right to be scared of him. If he had his way, they'd be taking a different kind of ride all together. He hadn't thought about anything else since he'd met her. Knowing she slept just a floor below him had him tied in so many knots he might never be able to unravel them all.

What the hell was wrong with him? She was just another woman. She had two arms, two legs, two eyes, a nose, a mouth, and various other parts that every other woman on the face of the earth had.

So what if her legs started at the ground and ascended to the clouds? So what if her waist looked small enough for his hands to fit around? So what if her lips were full and moist and surrounded a mouth made for kissing? That didn't mean she was different from any other woman.

But gut instinct told him she *was* different, and he'd always listened to gut instinct. It was the same sense that told him when a horse was trainable and whether it would do better as a cutting horse or a barrel racer. It told him when a cowboy who came around looking for a job wanted real work or just wanted to be trained for the rodeo by someone with a reputation.

His gut instinct rarely missed.

Damn. He didn't need this now. He needed to focus on selling the ranch. Spending time with Alex was just that much time away from organizing, making plans. He had a helluva lot more important things to do than chase after mouthwatering pie and incredible eyes.

Like fattening the stock so he could sell them if the buyers didn't want them. Like deciding what he wanted to take with him. Like getting back in shape for the rodeo. He still had a few good years left, even for rough stock.

He was so close. Travis was doing well on his own, and Claire would be leaving for college come September. Neither of them gave a damn about the ranch. Travis rarely came home, and Claire complained about ranch life constantly. Taxes were rising so high in this part of Wyoming, he was barely holding his head above water. He didn't know if he could pay Claire's tuition if he didn't sell it, and she was bound and determined to have a college education. He wanted to give it to her. She should have what she wanted.

But he should have what he wanted, too, shouldn't he? He'd given up his life to raise her and Travis. He just wanted that life back.

Dragging a heavy sigh from his lungs, he pulled himself up and opened Maisy's stall. He slipped on a halter and cross-tied her in the middle of the barn where the tack was stored. He slid a blanket across the horse's back, then topped it with an old, well-worn saddle that once belonged to his mother.

Pulling off Maisy's halter, Hank slipped a bit between her teeth and hooked the bridle over her ears. As he threw the reins over her neck, he spied Alex and turned to watch her moving toward the barn. She walked reluctantly, with stiff legs and a white face. Even so, he felt a familiar tightening below his belt.

Damn it! She wasn't the most beautiful woman he'd ever seen, so why did he want her so badly?

He must've been too long without a woman. He briefly considered driving to Riverton and renewing the brief affair he'd had with a widow there. But the thought left a bitter taste in his mouth. He didn't want Trisha. He wanted...

"What is it?" Alex demanded, coming to a stop just inside the barn. "You've watched every step I took across the yard without blinking, like I was—"

She blushed and turned away.

"Like you were what?" he prompted.

She gave him a narrow-eyed look, then lifted her chin. "Like I was stark naked."

Heat flashed through him. "Now there's a thought."

"Hank, I can't get involved with you. I'm headed—"

"To California. Yeah, I know." He cussed under his breath and turned back to the mare. "Don't worry, darlin'. I don't want to be tied down any more than you do."

"Good. I'm ready to ride the horse now."

As she walked around him to pat Maisy, he quickly reviewed all the reasons he couldn't have Alex.

It didn't do a damn bit of good. Every reason was airtight, but they didn't stop him from wanting her.

Hank knew Claire was coming across the yard as soon as the back door opened. Neither of them said anything as she settled beside him on the top plank of the corral fence.

Claire returned Alex's wave, then watched her circle a few times. "Are you sure this is Alex's first lesson?"

"That's what she said."

"Looks like she's ridden all her life."

"I wouldn't go that far, but she's doing all right."

"All right? Are you kidding? How many beginners can handle a lope at their first lesson?"

He shrugged. "She's got a natural rhythm most people forget they have. She tuned right in to the movements of the horse."

"How was school?" Alex called as she passed in front of them.

"Okay," Claire returned.

Alex was several lengths away before Claire bumped his arm and said, "You sound like a proud parent."

Hank would've cussed under his breath if it hadn't been so telling. He *was* proud of Alex, which made about as much sense as wanting her.

He settled his hat farther down his brow. "I didn't do anything to be proud of. Just sat her in the saddle. After thirty minutes I took off the lead rope, and ten minutes ago I came sat on the fence."

"Yep, you've got it bad. So—have you asked her to stay?"

"What in blue blazes are you talking about?" he asked a little sharper than he meant to.

"You know, stay with us instead of going to San Francisco."

"Of course not. And what do you mean, I've got it bad?"

Claire rolled her eyes. "Give me a break, Hank. You like Alex. It's as plain as the nose on Jed's face."

He turned his eyes back to Alex's figure and tried to sound

indifferent. "Of course I like her. You like her, too. Everybody likes her."

"Not in the same way you do," she said in a smug voice. "You *like* Alex. Like Ty Jordan likes me." She stuck a finger in her mouth like a mock gag.

"Don't be ridiculous," he spat.

"I'm not." She raised her voice as Alex passed them again. "The pot roast sure smelled good, Alex."

"Did you check it?"

"Yeah, it looked fine."

"Thanks."

Then Alex was past them.

"Of course, I don't know what a fine pot roast looks like," Claire muttered.

"Why not?" he asked. "You've eaten them."

"Yeah, but they were on platters, not in a pan. So, why haven't you asked Alex to stay?"

Hank did cuss under his breath this time. Claire was like a dog with a fresh bone. "She's got a much better job in California."

"But she wouldn't have us," Claire pointed out. Then she leaned closer. "She wouldn't have you."

"Claire…"

"She likes you, too, you know."

Hank knew he should cut the conversation off right there, but he didn't. "How do you know that?"

"Same way I know you like her. You look at one another like a calf looks at its momma. Like there's nobody else who'll do."

Hank shook his head. And he thought he'd been so good at hiding his feelings. If a teenager could pick up on it, everybody probably knew. "Don't be ridiculous. She's only been here a week."

"So?"

"She's leaving in three weeks."

"Well, that's my point. I think if you asked her to stay, she would."

Hank's eyes narrowed. "You want her to stay for your own sake."

"So? I've never had a sister. I've always been bossed around by you or Travis." Claire leaned against him. "But I'm not thinking only of me. You deserve somebody, Hank. You're getting too old and crotchety. Alex would be good for you. After all, a man has needs."

Hank stared at his sister in horror. "What the hell do you know about a man's needs?"

She rolled her eyes. "I'm not a kid, you know."

"You haven't—"

She hit his chest. "Don't be stupid. I'm not going to tie myself down to one of these dumb old cowboys. You, on the other hand, like it here on the ranch. So does Alex."

"She's leaving," he growled. "End of discussion."

*I'm leaving, too,* he wanted to add, *just like you're planning to leave, little sister. Just like Travis left.*

But he wasn't about to get into selling the ranch now.

His sister sighed. "Well, even if she does leave, you could enjoy her company while she's here, couldn't you? Aren't a few weeks of something better than nothing at all?"

Surprised at the tidbit of wisdom coming from his little sister, Hank turned his eyes back to Alex, who passed in front of them with a smile, but no comment.

Enjoy Alex while she's here. What a seductive possibility. It might even help get her out of his system, so when she did leave he could say goodbye with a fond smile. On the other hand, it might make it ten times harder to let her leave. There was just no way to know.

"So?" Claire prodded. "Why don't you ask her out?"

"You didn't see how she clammed up when I referred to this lesson as a date."

"So ease into it. You probably just surprised her. I know you, big brother. You're not exactly Mr. Subtlety."

For several long moments, Hank stared at the woman loping around the arena. "I'll think about it."

"You could start by taking a shower before supper. You and the hands smell like barn animals every night."

He shrugged. That's one thing he could do without making a commitment.

"And Hank?"

"Yep?"

"Don't think too long or she'll be gone."

That might be the best thing—for both of them.


Hank was waiting at the barn when the hands rode in from the north range. He lounged against the wide-open door while they unsaddled their horses and released them into the back pasture. When the three single hands walked out, he blocked their path.

"New rule, boys," he announced.

They stopped dead.

"Another one?" Derek quipped, earning an elbow in his ribs from Jed.

Hank gave Derek a quelling glance. "Showers before supper."

"What?" Buck cried.

"Shower before supper?" Jed bellowed at the same time.

"Are you plumb out of your mind?" Derek added.

"'Hat-head' and stocking feet aside, the ladies are offended by our odor," Hank explained. "You're not going to starve if you wait another fifteen minutes for chow."

"But we get just as nasty after supper as we do before," Buck pointed out. "When I jump to the ground with a piggin' string in my teeth, trying to wrestle a calf onto the ground, the dirt ain't gonna slide off just 'cause I done had my shower."

"That's right," Jed threw in. "Why, we'd have to take another one when we was done with practice."

"Then take another one," Hank said with no sympathy. "Getting wet twice in one day isn't going to hurt your thick hides."

"But boss—"

"We start tonight." Hank stared them all into submission, then turned on his heel. As he strode to the house, he heard muttered comments from behind.

"If that don't beat all. Two showers in one night!"

"First the hats and boots, now showers. There's a woman behind this."

"And we know who she is, don't we, boys? The boss put his brand on Alex the day she drove onto the ranch."

"Yep. He's been after her like a bull after a heifer in season."

"Poor boss. He's got it bad."

"Hell, it's about time. Maybe he won't be so mean."

"What kinda weed you been smokin', Jed?"

Alex had just flipped the first batch of corn bread from the iron pan onto the plate when the back door creaked open. Had she been so engrossed in supper that she hadn't heard the hands clomping across the yard? Usually she could hear them talking halfway from the barn.

Wiping her hands on her apron, she hurried to the door. "Y'all are early tonight. I'm not quite—oh, Hank." She stopped short.

He turned after placing his hat on the shelf. His blue eyes caught hers and held until every thought evaporated from her mind.

"You seem surprised to see me." He sat on the bench built into one wall and used the jack to pry off his boots.

"It's just that you're never the first one home. The hands always make it in before you."

He dropped the boots on the shelf under his hat and stood. Two steps brought him within inches. Alex backed up, but one step brought her against the doorjamb. She had to crane her neck to meet his eyes.

"Sorry if I upset your routine," he said in low, sultry tones.

Alex tried to swallow so the suddenly thick air could make it into her lungs. He stood so close his warmth reached out and surrounded her like a mink coat. That warmth and his musky, male scent fogged her brain, making it difficult to think.

"You didn't. I just...I mean I don't have a routine. I've only been here a week and—" She stopped as soon as she realized she was babbling. Sliding sideways, she stepped into the kitchen. "Supper won't be ready for another fifteen minutes."

He turned and started down the hall. "That's okay. I need to do something upstairs, anyway. The boys should be along about then, too."

Alex could no more stop her eyes from following him than she could stop them from following the path of a shooting star. When she heard the fourth stair creak under his weight, she snapped out of her trance and turned back to the stove, cursing herself for her foolishness. Why couldn't she keep herself from falling into his eyes every time he looked at her? Why couldn't she keep her breathing regulated or her pulse at its normal rate?

She didn't know. She only knew there was nothing she could do about it. She couldn't even work herself out of it—but she'd done her best. The downstairs rooms shone like new copper pans. She planned to start on the upstairs tomorrow if their trip into town didn't take all day.

With a sigh, Alex checked the last batch of corn bread. Finding it done, she flipped it onto the first one.

She'd also tried to talk herself out of her foolish infatuation, but that only made her think about him constantly, which didn't help. All she could do was ignore it and hope it would go away.

The swinging door between the kitchen and dining room flew open, and Alex's head snapped around.

"Sorry I'm late," Claire said breathlessly. "Want me to set the table?"

Alex looked down. She had a stack of bowls in her hands. Funny, she didn't remember getting them out of the cabinet. Shaking her head to clear the cobwebs, she held them out to Claire. "Sure."

Claire rattled on about something as she came in and out of the kitchen. Alex answered her absently, trying to concentrate on finishing supper. The hands wandered in a few minutes later, complaining among themselves, but she ignored them, too.

It wasn't until she set the last plate of corn bread on the table and stood back to make sure she hadn't forgotten anything, that she noticed the new "do" sported by each of the men. Instead of having a circle creased into their hair, it was slicked back.

Alex turned her wide eyes on Hank, who moved forward to pull out her chair. His hair was wet, too. "You're clean!"

Claire's head came up. She glanced around the table, then leaned toward Derek and sniffed. "It's a miracle."

"No, it ain't," Buck said. "It's—"

"It's manners," Hank interjected, quelling whatever Buck was going to say with a hard look. "We don't want to offend two such beautiful ladies with our stink."

Claire grinned like she was in on an amusing secret. "He must mean you, Alex. I've been sitting at this table for eighteen years—"

"Seventeen," Hank corrected as he pulled out Alex's chair. Still in shock, Alex sat down hard.

"*Almost* eighteen years," Claire amended. "And they've never cared about offending me."

Hank took his seat, then sent a penetrating gaze around the table. "Let's just say that the lesson Alex gave us in manners the other day sank in. Now, bow your heads."

Normal conversation resumed after grace, but Alex barely noticed. She automatically took portions of food as it passed around. While she pretended to eat, her eyes kept darting to the dark, handsome man at the other end of the table.

What he'd done—was it really for her?—blew her away. First the boots and hats. Now this. It was almost as if he were acknowledging that it was her kitchen, her dining room, where she made the rules. Waves of heat made her feel as if she were melting into the floor. Maybe it was just a tiny part of the world, maybe it was just temporary, but it felt good to have a place people thought of as hers.

Hank glanced up, then, and caught her watching him. His eyes locked with hers and wouldn't let go. Alex didn't know how long they stared, only that his hard, dark face somehow softened, only that her heart doubled its speed.

"I've got some news," Claire announced, breaking the trance. "Travis is coming in next week."

"He called?" Hank asked. His voice was even lower than usual.

Claire nodded. "An hour ago. He's in California this weekend, but he's going to enter the rodeo in Lander next weekend. He'll be here Wednesday."

Alex looked around at the hands' avid faces. They seemed to think a great deal of Travis.

Hank shook his head. "Why does he insist on riding for Frank Spindel every year? It means giving up Corpus Christi, which pays a lot more."

"You know why," Claire said. "Mr. Spindel gave Travis his first chance to ride a bull. Travis isn't going to forget that, even if he is the number four bull rider in the world so far this year."

Hank shrugged. "It's his money."

"Can we go see him in Lander?" Claire asked, her eyes pleading. "Travis asked if we wanted to, and Alex has never seen a rodeo."

Every head at the table swiveled toward her. Alex blinked.

"You ain't never been to a rodeo?" Derek asked as if she'd been accused of never breathing air.

She shook her head. "All I've seen is what y'all do in the corral every night."

"Shucks, that ain't nothin'," Buck said. "We're just practicing. You ain't seen nothing till you seen cowboys riding for money."

"Would you like to go?" Hank asked.

Alex met his eyes and felt heat color her cheeks at the intensity in them. "I thought you were busy on weekends, since Buck and Jed and Derek usually are gone to rodeos themselves."

"Rowdy and Casey can take care of things for one day," Hank told her. "Their wives keep them at home, anyway."

"Oh. Well, don't go just for my sake. But if you're going,

I'd be glad to ride along with you. I've seen so much practicing around here, I'd like to see the real thing.''

Hank nodded, then turned to Claire. "We'll go."

Claire beamed down the table at Alex. "You'll have fun."

Alex smiled back. "I'm looking forward to it."

# Chapter Five

"It's easy to tell you and Claire are related."

Hank took his eyes from the road to glance at Alex. She sat as close to the door as possible and hung on to the handle with both hands. "Because we look alike?"

"Because you drive alike. Did y'all inherit the 'Twenty Miles Over the Speed Limit' gene from your mother or father?"

Hank chuckled. "Father."

"You should do that more often, too," she said quietly.

Hearing a breathless quality in her voice, he glanced over to see her eyes on him, soft and warm. That heat traveled across the cab of the truck and filled his chest. He had to clear his throat before asking, "Why?"

"You're nice when you smile, but when you laugh, you seem almost human."

His lips curved at her teasing tone. "*Almost* human? You mean I'm not?"

"The ranch hands don't think so. They say you're a slave driver."

Hank felt his voice lower as he asked, "And what do you think?"

"I think...I think I want you to slow down."

Hank eased his foot off the gas. Why not? They had all day. "Better?"

Sighing her thanks, she relaxed and seemed to move away from the door without really getting any closer to him. She didn't trust him. That shouldn't be important to him, but the fact that her wariness rankled told him it was. He dropped his speed again, until it hovered near the limit. At this rate it would take two hours to get to Riverton. That meant four hours in the truck with a woman who acted as if he might bite her head off any minute.

In an attempt to get Alex to relax, he decided to try conversation. Since he was curious about how a Southern lady ended up in Wyoming, he started there. "So, you're from Alabama. Where about?"

He felt her look at him but kept his eyes on the road.

"A tiny little town in the southeastern corner called LaNett. It's as small as Dubois, I think. How many people live in Dubois, do you know?"

"The last census had us at around nine hundred, I believe. But the town's growing every day. People moving in from all over. It's..." Hank trailed off as he realized how smoothly she'd changed the subject from her to him. He'd noticed she did a lot of that. Was it on purpose? He decided to find out, and changed the subject right back. "It's a dadburn shame. I like it small. So this LaNett is just as small? You born there?"

"Born and raised. How about you? Where were you born since there's not a hospital in Dubois? Riverton?"

"No, I was born at the house."

"At the ranch house? Didn't your mother believe in hospitals?"

"Oh, sure, she just couldn't get there. A storm blew through the night before, and for once it didn't dump all its snow on the Tetons. There were four-foot drifts blocking the road into Dubois."

"She had a baby all by herself?" Alex pressed.

He threw a glance her way. She'd done it again, but she

seemed genuinely interested in his answer, so he continued, "No, my dad delivered me."

"You're kidding!"

"Nope. It's not uncommon for a rancher to deliver at least one of his children. He's usually had enough experience pulling calves and foals to know his way around…that end of things."

"What if there had been complications?" she asked in horrified tones.

He shrugged. "Luckily there weren't—with me or with Claire. But Dad took Mom to the hospital as soon as the road cleared, which was the next day."

"Claire was born in a snowstorm, too?"

"No. Mom went into labor one morning when Dad and I were out on the range. Travis was home, but he was only five. By the time Dad and I made it home, Claire was ready to be born. I think it was only ten minutes after we walked in the door."

Alex slowly shook her head. "That's amazing. Your mother must've been a very strong woman."

Funny, Hank had thought of his mother as tiny and fragile, not strong. Now he realized she probably just seemed tiny because he was as big as his dad. His father had treated her like a delicate flower, so Hank had, too. But she must've been strong—and not just physically. She'd put up with his father all those years. Him, too. "Yep, I reckon she was, at that."

"It must've been hard on you when your parents died."

"You know what happened?"

"All you told me was they drowned in a flash flood."

Hank spoke past the sudden heaviness in his chest. "One of our bulls was stuck in an arroyo on the south end of the property. They'd been out riding and tried to save it. The bull got out in time. They didn't. At least, that's what we think happened. When their horses returned to the barn without them, the hands found the bull at the top of the arroyo. They found Mom and Dad a few hours later, half a mile down."

Alex was quiet for a moment, then said, "You weren't home, were you?"

He shook his head. "I didn't find out until the next day. I was on the road between Mesquite and Abilene."

"And you felt guilty about not being there. Especially for your mother."

Hank turned wide eyes on her. "You *do* read minds."

"No, I read people. I've gotten pretty good at it over the years. I've had to."

Before he could question her about that, she hurried on. "I would like to have met your mother."

Hank tried to imagine Alex and his mother together. He found he could, very easily. "She would've liked you."

"She would've? Why do you say that?"

"From what I've seen, you're a lot like her. You work hard, learn fast, and stand up for yourself."

"Oh."

A silent moment passed before Hank tried changing the subject back to Alex. "Were you born in a hospital? If LaNett's the same size as Dubois, it probably didn't have a hospital, either."

"It didn't," she answered. "But we did have a doctor there. He had a clinic with a couple of rooms for things like that. He still operated it when I left."

"And when was that?"

"Six years ago. I was nineteen. When you were nineteen, you'd been on your own for two years already, hadn't you?"

Hank shook his head. Gleaning information from this woman was like trying to pull a bull through a calf chute. It just wouldn't come. And she'd accused him of being tight-lipped. Maybe if he talked about himself for a while he'd show her that he'd taken the advice she'd given him the other night to heart. Then maybe she'd relax and open up.

He shifted to a more comfortable position on the seat.

Talk about himself. Sure sounded easy. But it wasn't, not for him. Look at what a fool he'd made of himself the other night in the kitchen.

He slid a glance over to Alex. But she hadn't seemed to think he was a fool that night. Every time he remembered how she'd watched him with those hot honey eyes, and how she reached out to touch his hand...

As a familiar ache began to grow, Hank shifted again. He wanted her to look at him like that again. If talking about himself is what it took, that's what he'd do.

He started out with basic facts and intended to stick to those. But as the miles sped past, Alex dug deeper, and he soon found himself telling her about growing up under the harsh hand of John Eden, about using the rodeo to escape. By the time he pulled to a stop in front of McGuffey's Tack & Saddlery, Alex was so engrossed, she didn't seem to notice they'd stopped.

"So you left home to get away from your father?" she asked.

Hank pulled the emergency brake, then turned to face her. "It was half me leaving and half him throwing me out. We'd had some knock-down drag-outs before, but when I came home drunk after being gone for four days, he just about blew out the windows with his yelling."

"Sounds like you deserved it," Alex pointed out.

Hank rubbed his chin and felt several whiskers he'd missed. "Probably. I don't think he meant to make me leave, but I knew our relationship wouldn't get any better if I stayed. I was already pretty well known on the local rodeo circuit, and I wanted to go professional. So I quit school, lied about my age and became a card-carrying member of the PRCA." When she looked at him blankly, he said, "The Professional Rodeo Cowboys Association."

"Just like that, you turned your back on your family, the town where you grew up, your home. How could you do that? How could anyone?"

Her eyes were huge as they regarded him solemnly, accusingly. Confused by her apparent pain, he lowered his voice. "Many people do, Alex. Most people do to some degree. Leaving the nest is the most common thing in nature. You left home, didn't you?"

She shook her head, sending the sunlight that streamed through the back window of the truck bouncing along her unbound hair. His fingers ached to bury themselves in the deep brown silkiness.

"Not willingly. I—" She swung her face away from him and her eyes lit on the sign. "We stopped."

"About five minutes ago."

"Oh. I didn't notice."

He grinned. "Really?"

"I'm sorry for being so nosy, but I—"

"Don't apologize. So you didn't willingly leave home. What happened?"

"I didn't know we were going to stop at a tack shop. I thought we just came for groceries."

Hank shook his head. What was so awful about her childhood that she didn't want anyone to know? He'd started the conversation to pass the time, but suddenly it had very little to do with getting Alex to relax. He wanted to know everything about her—and he was determined to do just that.

"We come to town so seldom that when we do there's always lots of things to take care of," he told her. "I've got to pick up a different kind of bit for that sorrel I've been training, among other things."

He made no move to get out, however, and Alex glanced at him nervously. "Then shouldn't we go in if we've got so much to do?"

"In a minute. What made you leave home, if you weren't willing?"

Alex's brows attempted to meet, wrinkling the skin between them. "Don't you live by the Code of the West? Butch told me it frowns on people who ask too many questions about people's pasts."

"If that's true, why did you ask so many questions about mine?"

"I'm from the South. Down there, nosiness is a way of life. We like to know everything about everybody."

"If I answered your questions, don't you think it's only fair that you answer mine?"

"No. I mean..."

Fascinated, Hank watched as her face reflected her struggles with her sense of fair play.

Finally she faced him. "Why do you want to know about my past?"

He turned the question around. "Why did you want to know about mine?"

Color stained her cheeks and she looked away. "I'm from the South, remember? We're nosy."

"You told me a couple of days ago that I should open up and discuss things. Don't you practice what you preach?"

She tossed him a nasty look for that bit of logic, but he refused to back down. If it came to a stubborn contest, he knew he could outlast anybody.

"I...you're my boss—for the moment. The more I know about you, the better I'll be able to please you."

Hank shifted on the bench seat, thinking of several specific ways she could please him. Feeling parts of him stirring that had absolutely no business in this conversation, he cleared his throat and turned her argument back on her. "And you're my employee. The more I know about you, the more—"

"All right, I get the picture." She sighed heavily. "Do you want my life story now when we have so much to do? Why not wait for the drive home? There'll be plenty of time then."

Hank studied her averted face. She had a point, but he knew she would try to avoid the conversation then. "Are you so ashamed of your past?"

"It's not that exactly."

When she didn't continue, he pressed, "Then what is it?"

She huffed. "I don't want to be pitied! There, I said it. Happy now?"

"No. You haven't told me anything, as usual. Why would I pity you?"

"Because I was raised in an orphanage!"

Surprised as much by her vehemence as her words, Hank sat back. He'd read *Oliver Twist* and other stories about the horrors of orphanages, and he'd known kids who'd been adopted. But he'd never actually met anybody who'd been raised in an orphanage. At least, he didn't think so. Maybe he had and they didn't want to talk about it any more than Alex did.

He had a hundred questions for her. Did she know who her parents were? Did she ever want to be adopted? Did the orphanage feed her gruel? But he knew his questions would take a long time, so he said, "You're right. We'll talk about it on the way home."

Alex stared at him as he opened his door and walked around the truck. As he opened her door, she asked, "No reaction? No 'You poor thing' or 'I'm so sorry' or—"

"There are worse things than growing up in an orphanage. And didn't you just say you don't want my pity?"

"I just— Oh, never mind. Why don't you go in? You don't need me."

He reached for her arm. "Yes, I do. We're getting you a decent pair of riding boots."

"Now wait just a minute. I've seen catalogs around the house. Boots are over a hundred dollars, and those are the cheap ones. I can't afford—"

"You don't have to. I'm buying."

"What? Oh, no, you aren't. You've already advanced me enough to pay for my car. I'll be so far in the hole I'll never be able to leave." Her eyes narrowed. "Or is that your plan? You thinking of bringing back indentured servitude?"

Hank felt his jaw tighten at her accusation. "This isn't an advance."

She crossed her arms over her stomach. "I told you, I don't take charity."

He cursed under his breath. Now that she'd told him about the orphanage, he knew why. And he didn't blame her. But she needed these boots, and he was dead set on buying them for her. "This isn't charity. You've earned them by doing more than your share of work around the house. Even if you hadn't, you'll pay me back when you feed me and my men on the trail drive. But you can't feed us unless you learn to ride. And you can't learn to ride with those crummy little shoes you wore the other day."

Her chin rose a notch. "I did okay. You said so yourself."

"Yes, but you were on the gentlest mount at the Garden. What will you do when you've got a horse that won't go faster than a rough trot? You've got to be able to put some pressure on it, and you can't do that with those shoes."

"Then I'll ride Maisy all the time."

He shook his head. "Maisy's going on twenty. She's too old for hard work. I started you out on her because she's gentle, but if you do any real riding, you're going to have to use one of the other horses."

She continued staring at him belligerently. Though she didn't offer any more arguments, he could see the wheels working in her head.

Before she could voice them, he said, "I'm looking at it like another piece of tack I have to buy. It's equipment I need to run my ranch."

"You don't buy boots for any of the hands," she pointed out.

He shook his head. "That's not true. I've bought boots for a few down-and-out cowboys over the past eight years, and I know my father did."

Her eyes narrowed at being lumped in with all the other charity cases. Before she could draw breath to blast his statement, he hurried on. "You wouldn't expect to buy your own saddle, would you?"

That took her by surprise. "No."

"Then what's the difference?"

Her face said she saw a lot of difference. "It just seems like a frivolous expense since I'll only be using them for one trail drive."

He lifted a brow at still another reminder that she was leaving, but he wasn't about to give in. "Aren't you the one who offered to bring lunch to us when you learn to ride?"

"Yes, but—"

"Then you'll use them for more than one trail drive, won't you?"

Alex rolled her eyes, signaling her surrender. She swung her feet around and slid to the ground. "All right, all right. But nothing fancy."

"Nothing cheap, either." He closed the door to the truck. "I don't buy equipment often, but when I do, I buy quality."

She placed a hand on the horseshoe that served as the door handle for the store. "Then you pick them out. I don't know anything about boots."

He put his hand over hers and pulled the door open. Realizing he'd be holding her leg as he pushed on the boots, he grinned as she ducked into the store. "Darlin', that'll be my pleasure."

Alex wriggled her toes in her new boots as she waited by the café door for Hank to pay the check for lunch. He'd insisted she wear them today "to break them in." She couldn't remember owning any shoes like them. At first she found it hard to walk. The stiff brown leather came halfway up her shins, and the sole was reinforced with a steel shank so it didn't bend. That combined with the two inch heel made her feel like she was slapping the floor with every step.

But she had to admit they were sturdier than any other shoe she'd ever owned. She could probably kick the tar out of anything…including nosy bosses.

That thought made her look at Hank, who waited patiently for his change. She didn't know what to think about all the attention he'd been lavishing on her.

On the one hand, there were times when he looked at her like he wanted to rip off her clothes and devour her raw. She shivered as she remembered one particular look just that morning. She'd stood up to walk a few steps in the fourth pair of boots. She'd have been happy with the first pair—he was the one who insisted she try on several different styles. She'd studied herself from several angles in the boot-high mirror, then turned to find his eyes on her, hot enough to melt stone. She'd stood mesmerized, until he finally looked away.

But on the other hand, there was no real evidence Hank had any sexual interest in her. Just those looks making the air between them sizzle like a pan of fajitas. He didn't make passes, didn't try to kiss her. He treated her like he treated everyone else—and he was driving her crazy.

Hank unwittingly proved that by holding the door to the café open for her, then for a group of five women who were on their way in. He placed his hand on the small of her back as he walked her to the truck, but she'd seen him do the same with Claire.

As Alex climbed into the cab of the truck, she felt so frustrated by the unacknowledged tension that she wanted to scream, "Look if you want to sleep with me, let me know so I can leave now."

But she didn't say anything. Not only did she owe him for fixing her car, but if she were wrong, she'd feel like an idiot. So she just waited to see what his next move would be.

He drove straight to a supermarket three times as big as the one in Dubois and pulled up to the front door. "I need to check on a couple of things at the courthouse. Will you be okay for about an hour?"

"Sure. I've got a list a mile long."

"Add some gingersnaps to it."

"You like gingersnaps?"

"Yep." He leaned across to open the door for her. "Haven't had any in a while. Get me some, will you?"

"No." Alex hopped from the truck and turned to see his frown. "I'll buy ginger and make you some gingersnaps, but I won't buy stale cookies that cost three times as much."

There was that look again. Blue lasers.

Her body reacted the same way it always did—invisible shivers rippling across her skin. She grabbed the door to close it. "Anything else?"

He shook his head. "I'll catch up with you in an hour."

"Okay. I'll save the frozen stuff for last, since you'll have the ice chests. Do I need to ask about getting the dry ice now, or when we pay?"

"I'll take care of it," he said. "They know me here."

"Okay." Alex closed the door of the truck, then stepped back as he pulled away. It struck her that they interacted like a married couple.

She shook her head as she turned into the market. Married? Where had that notion come from? She was not in the market for a husband, lover or friend. She wanted to finish out her month, then head for San Francisco. Period. End of discussion. She was not listening to anything else her libido had to say on the subject.

Alex stood back as Hank and a young grocery clerk named Mike loaded the supplies into the bed of the truck. The more fragile supplies were packed in boxes, the sturdier ones in sacks, the frozen ones bedded down in the ice chests with dry ice. They'd spent an enormous amount of money, but Alex knew these supplies would feed six people for at least two months—if the right person was preparing it. She felt a twinge of guilt when she realized that person wouldn't be her, then rationalized that she would leave a well-stocked pantry for the next cook.

So the amount of money they'd spent didn't really bother her. The reason her mouth had gone dry was knowing what Hank expected of her on the way home. She'd been dreading it all day.

She chided herself for being so reluctant to share her past. But she couldn't forget the looks on co-workers' faces who treated her like everybody else before they knew she'd been an orphan. The change wasn't radical after they found out. They didn't treat her like a leper or anything. But she'd catch looks of pity on their faces when they caught themselves discussing all the family they were having over for Thanksgiving dinner or Easter or Christmas. They would invite her, and she would refuse, then they'd look at her with even more pity. Or relief, which was worse.

Little Orphan Alex. No one had actually called her that, but the name was too close not to make the comparison. She hated being different, hated being the one who never quite fit in anywhere, who never belonged.

"That's it," Hank announced after he tested the security of the tarp he'd tied on top of the groceries. He handed the clerk a tip, then turned to her. "You ready to head back?"

Alex nodded mutely and stepped toward the door. As usual, Hank made it there before she did and swung it open.

She expected him to light into her right away, but he hadn't said anything by the time they'd made it to the outskirts of Riverton, and she began to relax. Maybe he'd forgotten.

She should've known better.

As soon as he cleared the last subdivision, Hank pushed the truck into fourth gear to stay. He relaxed and stretched his arm across the back of the seat. "Now, where were we?"

Acutely aware of his every move, she knew his fingers were only inches from the back of her neck. Could she really feel their heat, or was it just her imagination? She stiffened away from his hand. "I was hoping you'd forget."

"Not likely. I just wanted to get through the traffic."

Her jaw set, Alex stared out the windshield as she said, "There really isn't that much to it. I was born in LaNett, Alabama. My mother died when I was eight years old, and because I had no other family I was taken in by the sisters at Saint Mary's Orphanage. When I was eighteen, I was supposed to leave, but the orphanage gave me a job cooking. It shut down the next year, so I had to leave. There. Not exactly what bestsellers are made of, but it's my life story."

Finished, Alex glanced at him, watching carefully for any sign of disgust or pity. The frown he gave her held neither, only mild frustration.

"Most people's lives wouldn't make a bestseller," he said. "But you left out a lot of details."

"Like what?"

"Like what happened to your father?"

Alex frowned back at him. He would want to know all the gory details. Well, he knew the worst. Why not? "My father died in Vietnam when I was a baby. We never saw each other, except through pictures."

"He was in the army?"

"Yes. He was one of those unglamorous 'grunts' they show in movies. He stepped on a land mine during some mission. I don't think my mother ever really knew where exactly. All she got back were his dog tags. I still have them."

Alex felt his arm shift along the back of the seat, but he didn't remove it. She found that strangely comforting.

"How did your mother die?" he asked quietly.

"She never was strong, not like your mother. To feed us, she worked in a textile mill in LaNett. They had a union there and she made pretty good money until she got sick. First it was just a cold, but she kept going to work until it changed to bronchitis. She couldn't get rid of it. She ran out of sick days at the factory and went back to work sick." Sadness Alex hadn't allowed herself to feel in years welled up. "It finally turned into pneumonia. That's what killed her."

"Didn't she go to the doctor?" Hank asked.

Alex nodded. "She just didn't have enough time to rest, to get over it. The whole process lasted about six months. By the time he put her in the hospital in Dothan she was too weak. She lingered there for a couple of weeks before she died."

"Then you were placed in Saint Mary's."

"Yes."

"Was it horrible?"

"We didn't have to eat gruel, if that's what you mean. No, it wasn't horrible. It's just that there were over fifty girls vying for the attention of three nuns and six day workers. I...I missed having the sole attention of a parent. Perhaps if I'd been younger when I went there, I might have fitted in better. I wouldn't have remembered how it felt to have someone who tucks you in at night and reads you a story. Not just any story, but the story you choose." Like that book about a house that went from being a farmhouse to one surrounded by city noise. She couldn't even remember the title, only that her mother read it to her as often as she asked. Alex swiped at a tear. "I'm sorry. I didn't mean to go on and on. And I certainly didn't mean to cry."

"Hey, I forced you to talk, remember? And you can cry all you want. In fact, I've got a shoulder that's not being used at the moment if you want to slide on over."

Alex couldn't keep herself from looking down the expanse of his arm to the shoulder he referred to. A blue and red western-style shirt covered it, making the broad expanse seem even broader. She was glad his eyes were on the road because she knew longing glowed through her tears. "Thanks, but I'm okay."

"You sure?"

She sniffled. "Yes. I'm a big girl now."

"Yeah, I noticed."

She frowned at him, wondering what he meant by that cryptic statement, but he ignored her as he concentrated on passing a slow car.

"I'm sorry your mother died," he said as he settled back in the proper lane. "It was rougher on you than—"

"I don't want your pity!"

"Hey, wait just a minute," he said pointedly. "This morning you said you were sorry my mother died. Were you pitying me?"

She blinked. "That was sympathy, not pity."

"Can't I sympathize with you? Who better than someone who's lost their mother, too?"

She had to think about that one. "Okay, I see your point."

"Why so defensive?"

"Because people treat you differently after they know. That's why I don't like to talk about it. I just want to be like everybody else. Is that so hard to understand?"

"Most people want to be different from everybody else, to stand out from the crowd," Hank said.

"Not like this," she told him. "They want to be famous for something they've done or said or made. They don't want to be an object of pity."

Hank nodded. "You're right. But I don't feel pity for you. Life has dealt you some pretty rough blows, but you seem to have risen above them. I mean, you didn't turn into an ax murderer. You aren't living on welfare. You haven't turned to drugs. I'd say you're doing pretty damn good."

"Oh, right," she said sarcastically. "Ever since I left the orphanage I've drifted from town to town and job to job. I'm such a success."

He shook his head vehemently. "You're planning to go study under that fancy chef, aren't you?"

"Yes, but that's just because I happened to be working for

his sister-in-law in Denver. He called asking if she knew someone who wanted to chop vegetables in exchange for training. I jumped at the chance.''

"Well, that's what I mean. You grab your opportunities. And when one job doesn't work out, you get up, dust yourself off and get another. That's what counts. It's like I tell the hands. It doesn't matter if that bronc has thrown you a hundred times, you gotta get up, dust yourself off and get on another. Hell, success in most things is ninety percent persistence. That's what you've got and, darlin', that ain't pitiful. Not in my book.''

Alex stared across the seat, dumbfounded by his intensity. His fervor touched her so deeply she couldn't tell how far down the feeling went. But she knew that the dynamics of their relationship had just changed. Her opinion of this man had just risen several notches.

Which wasn't good. Now it would be even harder to keep her distance.

She gave him a wry smile. "You sound like a Southern Baptist preacher at an all-day prayer meeting and dinner on the ground.''

He glanced over and returned her smile. "I do get wound up. The boys'll tell you it's my favorite soapbox. Fortunately, it's my only one.''

As he watched the road, her eyes roamed over his profile. The strong jaw, the jagged line of his nose, the intensity of his sky blue eyes made him look like a predator. "I didn't know you had a bit of preacher in you.''

His voice lowered to bedroom levels. "Darlin', there's a lot about me you don't know.''

# Chapter Six

A spicy scent hit Hank's nose as he entered the house after his Saturday morning chores. The smell stopped him abruptly, and the screen door banged against the seat of his jeans.

Alex left at five that morning, headed for Laramie with Claire and Mallory. So who was cooking? Had they changed their minds?

His nose led him into the kitchen where he was momentarily disappointed to find not Alex, but a slow cooker that sat on the counter next to the stove, plugged into the wall. A note sat in front of it.

Hank lifted the lid. Chili. He took a deep whiff, then replaced the lid and picked up the note.

> This should do you and Jed for lunch and supper if you can stand to eat that much chili. If not, there's leftover roast in the fridge for sandwiches.
>
> Alex.
>
>  P.S. There are cookies in the moose.

Hank shook his head. Didn't she have enough to worry about, chaperoning two teenagers on a long shopping expedition?

He pulled the moose-head-shaped cookie jar forward and lifted the antlers to reveal several dozen gingersnaps. The pungent aroma drifted up, mixing with the spicy smell of the chili. He grabbed three, replaced the top half of the moose's head, then popped one in his mouth. As he closed his eyes to savor the cookie, images of Alex filled his head.

What the hell was he going to do about her? He'd tried to ignore his feelings, but just thinking about her put zing back in his blood, something he hadn't even known was missing. The sensation reminded him of the feeling he got when he backed his horse into a chute. During the few seconds he sat, tense and still, with a piggin' string in his mouth, just before he gave the nod to let the calf loose, he could actually feel the blood pounding through his veins. At that moment anything could go wrong, and everything could go right.

Anticipation was half the fun—with calf roping and with women. He went about his chores quicker these days, knowing Alex's shy smile would be there to greet him when he walked in the door.

Hank popped the last cookie in his mouth and sighed as he pushed the swinging door open and dragged his heavy boots upstairs. He would rather take the moose to the back porch and settle in the swing, but he'd have to wait until he had the first load of clothes washed. He did laundry once a week— throwing his clothes into the bottom of his closet at the end of every day. But he'd rather ride a hundred miles of fence.

He entered his room without turning on a light, knelt, and reached into darkness. Expecting the usual knee-high pile of dirty clothes, he lurched forward until his hand hit hard floor. He felt around. Nothing but one pair of jeans, a shirt, underwear and socks. He dragged them into the dim light. They were the ones he'd discarded last night, after his shower.

He stood and finally turned on a light. All the shirts he'd worn during the past week were hanging in a neat row. They weren't even wrinkled like they usually were when he hung them up, having ignored them until they'd gone cold in the dryer. He didn't notice them that morning because he'd just reached in and grabbed the first shirt he'd laid his hands on, as usual.

Alex.

His eyes fell on the chest. He strode the two steps and pulled open the second drawer. His jeans lay neatly folded. He shoved it in and dragged open the next to find neatly stacked underwear.

Warmth filled parts of him he knew he should ignore. But he couldn't. She'd touched his underwear. The thought was enough to make him slam the drawer closed and open the next. His socks were matched and folded in pairs.

He closed the drawer, then sank onto the bed.

What the hell did Alex think she was doing? Cookies were one thing. Washing a man's underwear was damned intimate. It was something a wife would do.

Panic should be running rampant through him. But instead of feeling another rope tightening around him, tying him down, he felt like he could fly.

He propped his elbows on his knees and dropped his head onto his hands. That wasn't possible. The feeling was an illusion. He'd always hated doing laundry. He just felt free because he didn't have to do it today.

Hank stood with a frown. He wasn't satisfied with that explanation, but he wasn't about to delve any further into his feelings for Alex. The only thing he knew for sure was that he wanted to grab her and kiss her until they both had to come up for air. Thank God she wasn't there.

Beyond that, he didn't know what the hell he felt for her, but he had a feeling that in this case, ignorance was bliss.

When Hank came downstairs early the next morning, he heard Alex humming in the kitchen. She usually hummed when she worked alone, he'd discovered. He found the habit as endearing as the sound of the sweet, slightly off-key tune.

The smells of bacon and coffee were strong as he pushed open the door from the dining room to the kitchen.

"Morning," he said.

She turned from the stove and smiled at him. "Good morning. You're a bit early for breakfast. It won't be ready for about twenty minutes."

He stepped further into the room. "I thought I made it clear that you didn't have to cook breakfast this morning, since you used your day off to go with Claire. I know you got in late."

"Were you still awake?" she asked in surprise.

He nodded. "I didn't get up, because I knew Claire would think I stayed awake to check up on her."

Alex eyes sparkled. "Didn't you?"

He shrugged. He wasn't about to tell her that she figured in his worries as much as his sister. "Was the shopping trip successful?"

Her smile broadened. "Oh, yes, it was. She bought a beautiful blue dress that's going to be just perfect. You'll have to get her to model it for you."

"I will." He walked further into the kitchen until he stood beside her. "One more thing."

She looked up at him with questions in her eyes.

"You washed my clothes." He said it like an accusation, but that was on purpose.

Her chin lifted a fraction of an inch. "How do you know Claire didn't?"

He stepped closer, invading her space. "Did she?"

She struggled with that a moment, then shook her head. "I was vacuuming your room and they were in the way, there on the floor of your closet. I threw them in the washing machine so I could get to the dirt beneath."

"What were you doing in my room in the first place? Cleaning upstairs is—"

"Claire's job. So fire me," she said smugly.

He wanted to laugh, and choke her, and pick her up by her slender waist and swing her around in the air. Most of all, he wanted to kiss her. Instead, he stared into her defiant eyes. "Don't wash my clothes again, Alex."

"Or what?"

His eyes dropped to her mouth. "Or they'll be hell to pay…in more ways than one."

Neither of them moved—even to breathe—for a space of time that stretched into eternity.

Alex was the first to break free of the spell. She stepped back and tore her eyes from his. "Yes, sir!"

As he turned on his heel and left the kitchen, he heard her add, "Mr. Hell."

Alex switched off the vacuum cleaner suddenly and cocked her head toward the front window of the parlor. The rumble she'd heard above the roar of the vacuum wasn't a figment of her imagination.

Since visitors never came to the front door, she hurried to the kitchen and peered out the window.

The rig sitting in front of the barn looked like it was on steroids. The truck was fire-engine red and looked big enough to seat four cowboys, which meant about six regular people. The bed was long and widened to accommodate four rear tires. The matching horse trailer attached was big enough to drive her car right in.

This had to be Travis.

A tall, lanky cowboy hopped out of the cab and called to someone down the drive. A minute later Hank rode into view.

Alex was relieved she didn't have to greet the legendary member of the Eden clan by herself. Then she remembered the vacuum cleaner.

With a tiny "Eek," she started to run into the parlor to hide the incriminating evidence, but she stopped at the door. To heck with how Hank felt about her cleaning. If she wanted to vacuum or mop or wash clothes, she was going to do it and that was that. He could just get over it.

She returned to the window. The Eden brothers were unloading a couple of horses from Travis's rig. The men wouldn't be in for at least half an hour.

Should she go outside and welcome the wandering Eden? She wasn't exactly family, to go traipsing out there to greet him. This was when she felt the difference most keenly. Though every person at the Garden had made special efforts to make her feel at home, she wasn't a permanent part of the Eden family—and never would be.

Then she remembered Derek saying Travis would be driving straight through from Kansas, because of the horses. He must be tired, and if he were like every other cowboy she'd met, he'd be hungry.

Always confident in the kitchen, Alex set about making Travis a hearty late lunch. On second thought, she threw enough on for Hank. Cowboys could always eat.

The back door announced their entrance with a loud squeak as she flipped a minute steak. Wiping her hands on her apron, she turned toward the door.

"Something sure smells good," said a voice a few shades lower than Hank's.

"Looks like Alex saw you coming," Hank told his brother. "Hope you're hungry."

"As a bull in a blizzard," came the reply.

Then they filled the doorway. Hank swept off his hat as his eyes locked on to hers. Their gaze held several seconds, then he slapped his brother on the back. "Alex, this is my brother Travis. Bull rider, calf roper, all around cowboy. Travis, this is Alex Miller, our new cook."

Alex knew she could've picked Travis Eden out in a crowd. He was a younger version of Hank—tall as the Continental Divide with shoulders just as wide, eyes the color of the Wyoming sky, and long legs slightly bowed by constant horseback riding. There were only three differences that Alex could see—Travis seemed to be a bare inch taller, his hair was several shades lighter, and his jawline was so square, it might have been shaped with a blunt instrument.

Alex walked around the kitchen table and extended her hand. "Pleased to meet you, Travis."

Surprise still on his face, Travis met her halfway. "Well, I'll be hog-tied and branded. Someone sure made me look like the south end of a north-bound cow, and I know exactly which sister it was. Claire made me believe 'Alex' was an old cowpoke good for nothing but the chow wagon." He took her hand but instead of shaking it, he brought it to his lips. "I am more than pleased to meet you, pretty lady. Hank, why didn't you tell me the new cook was a rodeo queen?''

Alex felt warmth creep into her cheeks both at the compliment and the glint in his eyes. She pulled her hand from his. ''I'm not any kind of queen. I'm just the cook, the *temporary* cook.''

''Temporary? Hank, you mean you're gonna let this pretty lady go?'' Travis sniffed deeply. ''Smells like she's the queen of grub.''

Alex wrinkled her nose. ''What an ugly word for food.''

''Grub isn't an ugly word to a cowboy, sweetheart,'' Travis told her. ''It's what gets us through the day. And yours smells like the stuff cowboy dreams are made of.''

Alex waved him off. ''This is just something I whipped up because I figured you'd be hungry. Just wait until the meal I fix tonight. I'll have you drooling in your sleep.''

''Sweetheart, you don't have to cook to have me drooling. My tongue's hanging so far out now, you could wind it up and use it for a bedroll.''

Instinctively recognizing an irrepressible flirt—never to be taken seriously—Alex smiled at his outrageous statement. ''You must be tired after your long drive, Travis. Why don't you go freshen up? It'll be another fifteen minutes before this is ready to eat.''

''Thank you, sweetheart. I believe I will.'' He turned to his brother. ''You sticking around?''

Out of the corner of her eye, Alex saw Hank nod, then watch Travis leave after a few more bantering comments. Then Hank's eyes fell on her. As she sliced a loaf of freshly baked bread, Alex could feel them follow her every move.

Finally unable to bear the uncomfortable silence, she looked up and asked, ''What?''

Hank's eyes blazed across the kitchen. He opened his mouth to say something, then closed it. Then he jerked the brim of his hat down another inch, turned on his heel and left the room.

''Rudy Monroe offered me twenty-two thousand for that heeling mare I've been using,'' Travis told Hank over coffee.

They sat alone in the dining room, at opposite ends of the table. "He and I got a check team roping down in Ardmore. Said he'd never seen a horse so responsive."

Hank's brows lifted. "So why are you still hauling her around? That's the most we've ever been offered for a horse."

Travis shrugged. "I told him I needed to get your okay. You trained her."

"I remember Rudy being a damn good cowboy. Has he changed?"

"No, I wouldn't worry about selling her to him. I just wanted to clear it with you. We're partners in this, after all."

Hank leaned back in his seat and rubbed his jaw. He'd never thought of Travis as his partner, but what else could you call it? Hank trained roping horses and Travis took them on the road until someone bought them. It hadn't started out that way. Hank had given Travis a couple of roping horses when he'd left for the national circuit. Travis sold one nine months into the first season, gave Hank two-thirds of the money, and took another horse Hank had trained. The same thing happened again, then again, then again. They'd sold fifteen horses during the past five years. Nine of them went to the national finals with the cowboys that bought them. Four won championships.

"It's fine by me. Sell it to him."

Travis nodded. "I'll call him later. I think he's going to be in Phoenix."

Hank considered Travis's words. Partner. Could he work with a partner? He was used to taking charge, making decisions that affected the lives of those around him with precious little input from them. But, hell, this was his brother. Travis owned one-third of the Garden, though he showed very little interest in anything on it except the roping horses Hank trained.

Hank cleared his throat. "From now on, you make the decision whether to sell. I trust your judgment. Let's get the money when they're willing to part with it."

Travis stared at him for a long moment, then nodded again. "I will."

A comfortable moment of silence stretched between them

as they both sipped their coffee. Travis kicked out the chair next to him, reared back his own, and settled his boots on the seat. Fashioned from bright blue leather, the boots had yellow eagles and red flames dancing up the sides. Travis had always been the flashy Eden.

"Spindel having team roping this weekend?" Hank asked into the silence.

Travis shrugged. "He always does."

Hank leaned back and drummed his fingers on the table. "You want to enter with me?"

Travis's chair fell with a thud. He stared at Hank, open-mouthed. "You mean it?"

Hank gave him a hard look. "I always mean what I say."

"Sure, Hank. I know that." He frowned. "It's a PRCA rodeo, you know."

Hank knew what his brother was asking. Only card-carrying members of the Professional Rodeo Cowboys Association could enter sanctioned rodeos. He took out his wallet, drew out a card and tossed it down the table.

Travis picked it up, then looked at him in amazement. "You never let your membership lapse. Why? You haven't entered a rodeo since Dad and Momma died."

Hank shrugged and reached for his card. "Just never did."

"Hell, Spindel's gonna shoot into orbit when I tell him. The legendary Hank Eden making a comeback at his rodeo. Mind if I ask another why? Like—why now?"

Hank couldn't keep his gaze from wandering toward the stairs, where Alex and Claire had gone up half an hour ago. "I've been thinking about getting back in it."

Travis looked between him and the stairs. "Does this have something to do with the lovely Miss Alex?"

"Hell, no!" Hank cleared his throat to dull the sharpness. In a slightly more reasonable tone, he asked, "Why do you say that?"

"The men looked mighty shiny tonight—right down to their boots. Somehow, I don't think they cleaned up for my benefit. From that and from the way you've been acting, I'd say Miss Alex is more than just the new cook."

Hank swallowed the last of his coffee and furrowed his brows at his brother. "What do you mean?"

"Come on, big brother. You've done everything but put a brand on her."

Hank rubbed the back of his neck. He'd never talked about any relationship with his brother. Hell, he'd never discussed *anything* with his brother. Like Alex pointed out, he'd handed down edicts and expected them to be obeyed. But for the first time in his life he needed someone to discuss these crazy feelings with. Maybe if he talked them through, he'd see how stupid he was being and get over them. He sure couldn't discuss Alex with the hands. But Travis? Could he stop thinking of Travis as his baby brother and accept him as a friend and partner?

Hank took a long look at Travis, assessing him as a confidant. What he saw gave him a mild surprise. Sometime during the four years he'd been on the rodeo circuit, Travis had become a man. Why hadn't Hank noticed? Travis looked like their dad in pictures taken when John Eden was young—except Travis smiled.

*Open up,* Alex had urged him that night in the kitchen. With her it hadn't been so hard. With her there wasn't a history of acting as a surrogate father. And she'd be gone in a few weeks. Travis would be around the rest of his life. But maybe that was the reason he should confide in Travis. Travis was his brother, after all. And Hank couldn't think of anyone he'd rather have as a friend.

He leaned forward in his chair and cleared his throat. "She's driving me crazy."

Travis's brow shot up in surprise at this disclosure, but he recovered quickly. "Hell, I'd be worried about you if she didn't. A woman who looks like that, living here in the house with you?"

Hank's eyes narrowed. "What the hell do you mean by that? She's not that kind of woman, Travis, so you just keep your paws to yourself."

The younger brother held up his hands in defense. "Don't

go getting riled up. I don't want Alex. But you've sure got it bad.''

Hank ran a hand down his face. His anger subsided as quickly as it flared up. Jealous. Of his little brother. Damn, damn and damn again. He might be further gone than he'd thought. But he asked hopefully, ''So you think it's just a bad case of lust?''

''Hell, I don't know after that. Sounds to me like Alex has been doing a little branding of her own.'' Travis shifted in his seat. ''But what's the problem? It's high time you got married.''

''No!'' Hank winced at his own outburst. Bringing his voice back to normal, he continued, ''She's leaving in a couple of weeks. She's got a job in California, studying under some fancy chef. She's just here because her car broke down and she needed the money.''

''And you haven't been able to talk her out of it?''

''I haven't tried.''

''Why the hell not? What have you got to lose?''

Hank hooked an arm over the back of the chair. What did he have to lose? A shot at a world championship and a gold buckle along with it. The carefree life of a rodeo cowboy. The dreams of a lifetime. That's all.

But he couldn't tell Travis that without telling him about selling the Garden.

He frowned as he remembered Alex's advice about letting people know what was going on. And now he had an offer that he could definitely live with. But the real estate agent said they could get more, so why tell them until things were final? It would only be another month or so. His brother and sister didn't want to be bothered with the details of selling. Neither of them cared a hoot what happened to the ranch. They'd made that clear enough.

Hank ran a hand back through his hair. He should've known talking to his brother wasn't going to solve anything. Travis couldn't help the situation with Alex. Hell, nobody could. He was damned if he pursued Alex and would feel damned if he didn't.

"Hank? Travis? Y'all still there?"

Hank started as Alex's call sliced through his thoughts.

"We're here," Travis called back.

"Claire's on her way down."

"We're ready, beautiful lady," Travis said as they rose from the table and made their way to the bottom of the stairs.

Alex smiled down at him and amended, "Beautiful la-*dies*." She descended the stairs with the air of a princess. When she reached the bottom step, she turned with a flourish of her arm. "I now present the charming, the brilliant, the beautiful...Claire Eden."

After a breathless moment, a vision appeared at the top of the stairs, dressed in a floor-length gown of deep blue that rose from a wide, flowing skirt to a sleeveless bodice that closely fit generous curves. Claire's dark hair had been swept up into an artful arrangement of curls and her face made up to perfection. She looked down on them with a half-haughty, half-uncertain expression, this angel that was his sister.

Hank was amazed. Just like his brother had grown up without his having noticed, so had Claire. Seeing her now, Hank had no doubt she was a woman.

"I thought you said Claire was coming," Travis said to Alex with a near-serious expression. "Aren't you going to introduce us to this lovely lady?"

Claire's face broke into a flattered, flustered grin. "It's me, Travis. I think."

"Of course it's you," Alex insisted. "You're beautiful."

Claire descended the stairs like a beauty queen. When she stood next to Alex, she lifted her eyes to Hank's. "Is it okay?"

Hank felt his throat choke at her nervous question. "Honey, it's perfect. You're perfect." He extended his hand. "May I have the first dance?"

"What—now?" Claire asked.

"Why not, kiddo?" Travis threw up his hands. "Does the stereo work?"

Claire nodded. "Alex and I have been wearing out Mom's old Patsy Cline records while we clean."

"I've got some tapes in the truck. Be back in a sec."

Hank offered one arm to Claire, who took it with a smile, then the other to Alex, who shook her head, blushing. Determined, Hank stood patiently with his arm extended.

Claire looked behind him. "Come on, Alex. It'll be fun."

Alex shook her head. "No, this is a family moment. I'll be in the way."

"You think I'm going to be the only one dancing with these two?" Claire asked. "Oh, no. When cowboys want to dance, they dance until their partners drop. You're coming, and that's that."

Alex sent a worried glance to Hank, and he smiled to reassure her. "You heard the lady. You're not getting out of this."

When Alex hesitantly put her hand on his arm, he escorted them into the parlor, then released them to push the furniture against the walls. Travis returned a moment later, handed a couple of tapes to Claire, then bent to help Hank move the heavy couch. By the time the dance floor was clear, Claire had found a lively tune on one of Travis's tapes. Hank bowed formally to his sister, then swung her around the room.

Alex watched them with hungry eyes, just before trying to slip out. No matter what they said, this was a family affair, and she didn't belong. She swallowed the lump rising in her throat. Would she ever belong anywhere?

Travis caught her hand. "You weren't thinking of leaving, were you?"

"I...I was just going to check on Sugar. He's—"

"Fine," he finished. "So you're going to dance."

"But I—"

"No excuses." Travis changed grips on the hand he'd captured and slipped an arm around her waist.

She shook her head. "But I don't know how."

"You can't do the two-step?" Travis gave her a disbelieving look. "Every five-year-old in Wyoming can do the two-step."

Alex turned her head to see Hank spin Claire under his arm. "Well, I'm a lot older than five and I can't. So let go please."

He shook his head. "Nope. It's my patriotic duty to teach

you. It's simple. Only two steps. Watch Hank and Claire for a minute. Okay, you two, enough fancy stuff. Do the basic steps so Alex can see. Look—slow step, slow step, quick step, quick step.''

"It's easy, Alex." Claire laughed as Hank twirled her. "And fun!''

Travis positioned his arms. "Come on, let's try. You go back, I go forward. I start with my left foot, you with the right. Now.''

Alex was grateful that Travis went slow because she had to count each step and look at her feet every fourth one. They made a slow circle around the room while Claire and Hank swirled around them, watching and calling encouragement. Knowing three pairs of eyes stayed on her made concentrating twice as hard.

"They're not doing the same dance we're doing," Alex said after Hank pulled Claire around until they were both dancing forward, their arms entwined.

"Yes, they are," Travis told her. "They're just adding some spark to it. Once you get the hang of it, you'll be able to do the same thing.''

"Right. That'll be when chickens flour themselves and jump in the frying pan.''

Travis laughed. "You're not doing bad.''

"I hope your toes say that tomorrow. Thank goodness the song's over.''

Travis caught her as she tried to escape. "Where are you going?''

"I danced, didn't I?''

"But now we change partners." He put her hand in Hank's and took Claire's, all in one fluid motion.

That quickly, Alex stood within the circle of Hank's arm. Shock kept her still, as warmth swept through her.

"Have fun," Claire told her as another up-tempo song began. "Hank's a better teacher than Travis.''

Travis swept her away. "That's loyalty for you.''

"Well, he is." Claire looked up into his handsome face adoringly. "But you're a better dancer.''

Travis grinned down at his sister, and Alex pulled her eyes away from their happy faces.

"You ready?" Hank asked quietly. "Remember to start with your right foot."

Hank stepped forward a second before Alex stepped back. His boot toe barely missed her shin as he lurched forward, catching her against him.

Alex tried to pull away. "I can't dance."

Hank wouldn't let her escape. "That was my fault, Alex. I'm sorry. Let's try it again, okay? Look at me." He held her until she met his gaze. "Okay?"

She dropped her eyes to the third snap on his shirt and nodded miserably. She felt like a cow in a roomful of ballerinas.

He loosened his hold. "Ready? Now."

They stepped in unison this time and Hank guided her around the room. Novice that she was, she still had to count and look at her feet. The third time she looked down Hank tightened his hold. She gasped softly as he fit their bodies so close together that she was stepping between his feet and he was stepping between hers.

"Don't," she breathed.

"You were looking at your feet."

"So?"

"You'll never learn to dance that way," he whispered next to her ear. "Close your eyes. Listen to the music. Feel me move. Don't worry. I won't let you bump into anything. Just move with me."

Alex had no choice but to comply. Her eyes wouldn't stay open as his warm breath tickled her ear, burning every thought from her brain. With her vision gone, other senses became acute. With every breath she inhaled Hank's light musky odor mixed with the even fainter smells of coffee and soap. His deep voice whispered soft words of encouragement. The music poured into her ears and went directly to her muscles, making them move with the rhythm. She could feel Hank from the beard scraping her forehead to the sculptured planes of his chest to the steely strength of his thighs moving against hers.

At that moment in time, Hank became her universe. Nothing else existed.

The song ended, but Hank kept on dancing. Alex was vaguely aware of Travis and Claire moving away, but she didn't want to open her eyes and break the enchantment. Hank wove a spell so drugging that it lasted the few seconds until the next song began. He adjusted their steps to the slower beat and began humming the tune. The deep sound reverberated through her, hypnotizing her, dragging her deeper into the depths of desire.

Another song began and ended, then another. Still they danced. Alex still heedless of time or company. Heedless of everything but the warmth that surrounded her, the comfort of the strong arms that guided her as she floated around the floor.

Finally the tape ended with a solid click. By slow degrees, Alex became aware of the silence that surrounded them. They were alone. Travis and Claire had left. But Alex didn't care. The music still echoed in her mind, and warm strength still surrounded her.

She vaguely remembered that there was some reason why she shouldn't be where she was, but she pushed that away, too. The only thought that mattered at that moment was the overwhelming sense that she was precisely where she belonged.

"You're a quick learner," Hank whispered.

Alex moaned softly, sad to realize the moment was about to end, that reality was about to intrude. In an effort to keep reality at bay, she rubbed her cheek against the soft chambray of his shirt and whispered, "You make it easy."

Hank moaned, too, and pulled her tighter against him. As he did, she realized that at some point he'd slipped both arms around her.

"Alex, look at me."

She shook her head, ignoring his quiet command. "Can't we stay like this for a while?"

With another moan, he brushed her hair from her neck and placed his lips in the hollow just below her ear. "Do you like being close to me?"

"Mmm."

He released a deep, ragged breath. "I like being close to you, too."

"You do?"

"Yes."

Alex knew something was wrong with that statement, but couldn't waken enough brain cells to analyze it.

"Alex?"

"Hmm?"

"I want to kiss you."

"You do?"

"Yes."

"Will it be nice, too?"

He groaned. "It will be even nicer."

By slow degrees, Alex levered her head so she could see him. His dark face hovered so close above her own she could barely focus on his features.

Before she could say anything else, his lips touched hers. The word *nice* flew from her head and other, more sensual terms replaced it—all having to do with heat—*searing, burning, scorching.*

The warm lassitude accompanying their dance fell away, replaced by a fervent desire to burn him as fiercely as he was burning her. She dug her hands into the short spikes of his hair, pulling his lips close enough for them to meld.

"Damn, Alex," he breathed against her mouth. "I never thought—"

His tongue traced her lips, then slipped inside. Alex felt the impact in her toes as wave after sensual wave cascaded down her body. With a moan coming from deep in her throat, she touched her tongue to his. His hands dropped down to her bottom and pushed her against a hard, pulsing ridge.

Alex froze as reality finally flooded back.

"Stop!" she cried, ripping her mouth from his. Hot tears stung her eyes as she tried to pull from his embrace. "We can't."

Lost in his own sensual fog that had thickened considerably since they stopped dancing, Hank reflexively held on to Alex, despite her struggles. She'd changed so quickly from a warm, wonderful armful that it took a moment for his dazed mind to realize what had happened.

"What's wrong?"

"Let me go!" she cried. "I can't do this."

Struck dumb by her tears, he let her go. She ran down the hall, and a moment later the screen door at the back slammed shut.

Raking fingers through his hair, he fell back. Instead of hitting the chair usually there, he sat hard on the coffee table, but he was beyond caring.

What the hell just happened? What started out as a celebration of Claire's womanhood had ended up as a seduction of Alex.

No, that wasn't true. Alex had been a willing partner in everything, up until the last moment when he…when he what?

When he showed her exactly how much he wanted her.

Damn.

And damn Travis, too. During the third song, his brother pulled Claire out of the parlor with a broad wink. At that particular moment, Hank had been so enmeshed in Alex's spell that Travis's scheme barely registered. Now he could cheerfully put his fist through his brother's smiling face.

Hank shook his head. It wasn't Travis's fault, it was his. If he hadn't told Travis he was attracted to Alex, this wouldn't have happened.

But it had happened, and somehow Hank couldn't bring himself to be sorry. Hell, all he'd done was kiss her. What was so wrong with that? Eyes narrowed, he looked at the door Alex had escaped through. She'd certainly found something wrong with it, and he intended to find out what.

# Chapter Seven

Hank found Alex easily, sitting on top of the corral fence, staring at the full moon and shivering in the cool night air. He knew the moment she realized he was coming because she stiffened, then pulled her heels from the third rail as if about to jump down.

"You might as well stay right there," he called. "Because I'm coming after you. You can run all the way back to Alabama, but you'll feel me breathing down your neck."

She didn't say anything until he stood at the fence.

"Just leave me alone."

"Hell, no." He climbed up and straddled the top rail, facing her. The moonlight bathed her face with an ivory light that traced the path of a tear. His voice softened. "What did I do wrong? Kiss you?"

"Yes!"

"I asked, remember?"

"I didn't say yes."

"Not with your lips, but every other part of you was screaming yes."

Her wince admitted she knew he was right.

"Are you saying you didn't want me to kiss you?" he asked.

For a moment she looked like she would deny she'd wanted his kiss, but she didn't say anything.

"You can't say it, because it isn't true."

"I didn't!"

"Don't lie to me," he said softly. "I was on the receiving end, remember? You pulled me closer, wanting more."

With a choked sound, she leaned over until her head rested on her knees. "No, it isn't true! It can't be."

Wanting to comfort her, Hank stretched a hand over her back. But he stopped short of touching her. "Why not? What's wrong? Tell me."

"I'm leaving, that's what wrong. I have to go to San Francisco. That job is a once-in-a-lifetime opportunity. If I don't go now, I'll never get another chance. Then I'd never be able to open my own restaurant. Then I'd never have…"

"Never have what?" he prodded gently.

She looked at him with tortured eyes, making him ache to draw her into his arms. "You wouldn't understand."

"Try me."

She shook her head vehemently. "How could you? The Garden has been here for you and your family for a hundred years. Even when you left it to rodeo, you always knew you could come home, that there was someone here who cared about you, who gave a damn whether you rode your bronc or if it trampled you in the dirt."

Suddenly everything became crystal clear. Her mother dying, the orphanage, drifting from place to place—she needed a home, a family.

She needed exactly what he couldn't give her.

A few months from now, the home she thought so permanent would belong to someone else—probably would be bulldozed to make way for a new subdivision. Even if he didn't want to return to the rodeo, he'd have to sell the ranch sooner or later. The ledger didn't lie.

Pain swept through him, so sharp and deep it nearly knocked him from the fence. He wanted to be the one to give her what she needed. He wanted to be the man she kissed goodbye every morning and hello every evening. He wanted to sit on the swing with her in the crook of his arm and watch the sun go down. He wanted to sleep with her at night, to help her deliver their children, to grow old with her. But he couldn't.

The realization he'd had earlier hit him again. He was damned if he got close to Alex, and damned if he didn't.

So—if he was damned, anyway, why not take Claire's advice and make the most of the time he and Alex had? The reality of her going couldn't hurt any worse than the thought of it did right now.

Very slowly, as if he were approaching a skittish mare, Hank reached over and pushed an errant strand of hair behind her ear. "I know you're leaving. I understand. Believe me, I do. But damn it, Alex, I don't want you to be afraid of me."

Her arms crossed over her midriff. "I'm not afraid of you. I'm afraid of the way you make me feel. I can't start any kind of romance with you. If I do, I might never go to San Francisco. And that's something I'll regret the rest of my life."

Hank searched her eyes in the moonlight. "And if I let you go without finding out what this is between us, I'll regret it for the rest of my life."

He didn't realize he'd said it out loud until her eyes widened. The words scared him almost as much as they scared her, but he'd be damned if he'd take them back. He scooted closer. "Look at me. Please... Alex darlin', I can't promise you anything—certainly not forever. All I know is that I've never felt this way about any other woman."

She stared at him until he thought he'd start howling at the moon. Finally she asked, "What are you saying?"

"I'm saying I want to spend time getting to know you, letting you get to know me." He reached out and placed his hand over hers. He was gratified when she didn't pull away. "Be my date at the rodeo this weekend."

She stared at him a long minute, then shook her head. "I don't think that's a good idea."

"Why not?"

"I'm leaving in two and a half weeks, Hank. I have to do this."

"I know. I'm not asking for a lifetime commitment. Just a date. We'll have a few laughs. I'll hold your hand, buy you a barbecue supper and claim all your dances at the hoedown after the rodeo."

She pursed her lips and shook her head again. "No. We shouldn't."

Hank's hand tightened in frustration, but he kept his voice low and calm. "Can you honestly say you could leave now with no regrets? Without ever wondering what it would be like to kiss me?"

"I know what it's like to kiss you," she said in husky tones. "That's what started all this, remember?"

"Can you tell me you don't want to do it again?"

"Yes."

"Liar."

She quickly looked way. "Damn your cowboy hide."

Heat surged through him, making him want to drag her back into his arms. But knowing he had to tread carefully, he ignored it.

"When I was ten, just starting out in rodeo, I'd drawn a bucking horse that nobody but the best professional cowboys had ridden. That mare bucked off every kid that I knew, and hurt a lot of them, one real bad. Anyway, I was going to draw out. I didn't want to get hurt bad enough that I couldn't rodeo anymore. One old hand, Tex McQuire, came up beside me as I was standing by the pens, staring at that rank old mare. He asked why I wasn't going to ride. I told him I didn't want to be sorry the next day. To make a long story short, he made me realize that I'd be sorry if I didn't ride her. I ended up climbing on the back of that old mare, and I made the whistle.

"That's how I've lived my life ever since. If I know I'm going to be sorry anyway, I want it to be for something I've done, not for something I didn't do. Do you understand what I'm saying? Since we're going to be sorry whether or not we spend time together, why not make some memories to soften the blow?'' He laced his fingers through hers. "Go with me this weekend.''

"I'm already going.''

"Go as my date. There'll be lots of people there. You'll be as safe as a chick in the nest. And we'll have Claire and Travis to chaperone. But I want the right to hold your hand...like this. I want to put my arm around your waist...like this.'' He drew her against him. "I want the right to kiss you good-night.''

Alex slowly relaxed against him. "Damn you, Hank Eden. How can I resist you when you say things like that?'' She released a long, miserable sigh. "But I have a feeling we're going to regret it.''

Damned or damned? With Alex in his arms, the choice seemed a lifetime away.

Claire and Alex arrived in Lander, hauling an empty horse trailer behind Hank's red pickup. The brothers had left several hours before them so they could pay their entry fees and settle down their horses after the two-hour ride. They went separately because Travis wouldn't be going back to the Garden. He planned to spend the night in Lander and head for Texas the next morning.

Claire guided the truck over the rough field that served as a parking lot for the small-town rodeo. Alex breathed a prayer of thanks that she went slowly because of the children chasing one another amid the cars, trucks and horse trailers filling the lot.

"Judging from the number already here, I'd say they're going to have a good crowd,'' Claire said. "I know they've heard Travis is riding today. He comes every year. I wonder if it's gotten out that he and Hank are joining up for team roping.''

Alex pointed to the entrance of the arena. "I think that answers your question.''

Under a weathered sign telling spectators they could watch "Travis Eden—World Champion Bull Rider and All-Around Cowboy,'' hung a new banner that read: "See Hank Eden— Riding and Roping Again after Eight Years.''

Claire gave Alex a wry look as she killed the motor. "I should've known Mr. Spindel wouldn't let it slip by. These small-town rodeos make a big deal out of having one big name. Having two will probably fill the arena. Which, of course, isn't saying all that much. You ready to go find your date?"

Claire seemed certain this "date" meant Alex would stay on as cook, ignoring Alex when she insisted she was still going to San Francisco.

Alex took a deep breath. "I guess I'm as ready as I'll ever be."

"Let's go."

As they left the truck, Alex spied a coiled rope, partly braided, in Claire's hands. "What's that?"

She smiled as she held it up and started for the arena. "Our ticket behind the chutes."

They made their way through the parked cars and people. Alex returned the smiles and nods of welcome. Several people called to Claire, but she didn't stop to talk to anyone. Instead, she guided Alex to the back of the arena.

As they got closer, Alex recognized the pungent odors of earth and animals. They passed a low, flat-topped frame building with crude letters above a white door proclaiming it the rodeo office. Late-arriving cowboys and their families milled around the outside, looking over the program or catching up on the latest news and gossip.

Alex tried to hide her relief when the gray-haired cowpoke guarding the gate announced there was no entrance to anyone but paid participants. Claire showed the guard their "ticket" and pleaded with him to let her give her brother the favorite bull rope he had left at home by mistake. The guard was unmoved, even when Claire mentioned who her brothers were.

Alex took Claire by the arm. "We can see them after the rodeo."

"We might not live much past that," Claire told her miserably. "At least I won't. This really is Travis's favorite bull rope. I took it out of his trailer after they loaded up the horses."

"Why would you do something like that?"

"I wanted Hank to see you before the rodeo."

Alex closed her eyes and shook her head. "Claire, Claire, Claire."

"Well, there are a lot of buckle chasers hanging around rodeos, and I wanted to remind him he already has a date."

"Claire…"

"I want you to stay and be my sister," she declared, her chin set.

Alex's eyes widened. "Sister? How many times do I have to tell you? I'm going to San Francisco. Nothing is going to stop me."

Claire shook her head as she scanned the people milling around the rodeo office. "I've never seen Hank act this way. He'll stop you."

"Claire!"

"So sue me."

Alex let out a huff of frustration, then suggested. "Why don't you give the rope to someone who has paid their entry fee so they can give it to Travis? You know enough people here, surely you can find someone."

"That's not the point. I—" Claire's face suddenly brightened, and she ran forward, waving. "Mr. Spindel!"

Five minutes later the rodeo sponsor escorted them through the gate himself. Claire smiled prettily at the guard, who watched them go past with narrowed eyes.

"Now just ten minutes, Miss Claire," Mr. Spindel told her. "It's not safe back here with all the livestock being moved around."

"Oh, yes, Mr. Spindel. We'll be out quick as a wink! Thanks so much. You've saved my life!"

Alex shook her head. Claire knew cowboys well, especially how to twist them around her little finger. She'd be at home with the best Southern belles.

Claire led them through a maze of plank fencing, past rows of narrow pens, some filled with calves, some with horses, some with bulls, some empty.

The cowboys milling about came in all sizes—short, medium, tall and kid-size. Nearly all had the same build: broad shoulders, narrow hips, strong legs. They all wore the same uniform: cowboy hat, boots and blue jeans. The only difference between them were their long-sleeved shirts, which varied in hue from soft neutrals to bright stripes to vivid solids appliquéed with various Western items like horseshoes or Indian feathers.

Most stood around in groups talking, but as they passed through, Alex saw a few sitting on their saddles, checking the length of the stirrups. One cowboy stood alone in an empty pen, going through the motions of riding. Still others threw lariats at handmade dummies of steers.

Regardless of what they were doing, however, all the cowboys stopped to watch Alex and Claire pass by.

Distracted by the attention they received, Alex bumped into Claire when she stopped suddenly and planted her hands on her hips. "I knew it."

Alex followed her gaze to a group of cowgirls. In the middle, their height unable to hide them, stood Hank and Travis. "I thought women weren't allowed back here."

"They're barrel racers," Claire said in disgust. "I know a couple of them."

Seeing Hank's animated face smiling at the young women, Alex had a sudden urge to scratch the makeup off their pretty young faces.

A sick feeling of horror swept over her. She was jealous. Dear sweet— She was a lot farther gone than she'd thought. Damn Hank. She didn't belong here. Not as his date. Not as anything.

She began her retreat a second before a bellow stopped her. "Alex, wait!"

She turned to see Hank pushing his way through the passel of young admirers. As he came out, Claire started down the path he'd cleared to Travis. Alex made a grab for her, but missed.

Hank's eyes didn't miss an inch of her as he moved forward. His smile widened as he met her eyes. He stopped so close she had to crane her head to peer up at him. The brim of his hat shaded her face as well as his own.

"You look great," he said quietly.

Alex looked pointedly away. "Thanks."

He caught her chin and tilted her face back to his. "What's wrong?"

"Nothing." Alex tore her chin away and took a step back.

He stepped closer. "Damn it, Alex, you were fine this morning."

"You weren't surrounded by a bevy of young cowgirls this morning." She regretted the words as soon as she said them. The last thing she wanted was for Hank to realize she was jealous.

He picked up on it immediately. She could tell by the way his intense blue eyes searched hers. Suddenly he grabbed her hand and pulled her into an empty pen. The gate closed behind them. He backed her up against the planks, leaned on one arm and ran his free hand along her cheek. "Thanks for coming to see me."

He was so close, his soft, warm breath fanned her cheek. Alex gazed into his shadowed face. Feeling herself falling under his spell, she ducked away.

He caught her arm.

She glanced back. His hold on her arm wasn't strong or confining. She could pull away anytime. But she didn't. "Claire had to give Travis a bull rope."

"He forgot it? That's not like Travis."

Alex shook her head. "Claire stole it out of his trailer."

Hank smiled wryly. "Looks like we don't have to worry about the family's approval."

"For what?"

"For anything we want to do," he said softly.

Suddenly Alex found it hard to breathe. "I'd better go. Mr. Spindel gave us just ten minutes to find you."

He slipped his hand down to hers and ran his thumb over her palm. "How about a kiss for luck?"

Alex caught her breath and glanced between the rails of the pen to the cowboys beyond. No one was paying them the slightest attention. It was as if they'd disappeared when the gate closed on the pen. She shouldn't give in to Hank's request. But his breathless words, the sensuous touch on her hand beguiled her, and—God help her—she wanted to taste him again.

"All right," she said softly. "For luck."

His face turned serious. He stepped closer and leaned down, his eyes holding hers until his mouth made contact. He used just the slightest pressure. The kiss was lingering, sweet. Still, her heart raced like Hank's truck engine did under his heavy boot.

He pulled away and their eyes met. "Don't look at me that way, or I'll be kissing you the way we kissed the other night."

Her eyes drifted down to his mouth. "I wouldn't mind."

He groaned. "I wouldn't either, darlin'. But if we do, I won't be able to leave this pen for a while. My pants are tight enough already."

Alex felt her cheeks sting as she realized what he meant.

"But I'll take a rain check, if you don't mind." His eyes burned into hers. "Tonight when we get home."

Alex felt the heat in her cheeks fill her entire body. Home. What a beguiling word. What would it be like to call the Garden her home, the Edens her family? To cover her longing, she stepped back and gave him an arch smile. "I'm not promising anything, Hank Eden. You stay away from those barrel racers, and we'll talk."

He grinned as she pushed open the gate. "What barrel racers?"

"Ladies and gentlemen! This is the moment we've all been waiting for! The legendary Eden brothers from right here in Wyoming are setting up as the fourth contestants in our team roping event. Buckaroos, this is a first not only for the Spindel rodeo, but for the world. Hank Eden is a Wyoming legend and Travis Eden is the current World Champion Bull Rider and All-Around Cowboy. They are teaming up for the first time ever for this event. We are proud to have them at our arena…"

Applause, cheers and whistles drowned the announcer's voice as Hank and Travis rode into the arena. Hank spared a glance at Alex and Claire, whom he'd spotted in the crowd while waiting behind the chutes during the early events. Then he tuned out all the noise. His old competition habits were coming back. They were almost as good as when he'd shoved them into a closet in his mind eight years ago.

He glanced at Travis, who nodded, then he guided his horse into the header's box. He turned the horse around and backed him into the far corner. On the other side of the chute, Travis mirrored his actions in the heeler's box. Between them, the steer clanked into the chute. The Hereford-mix had leather sleeves wrapped around the base of its horns to protect them. They were wide and evenly curved, a good target.

With a deep breath to appease the adrenaline pounding through him, Hank mentally checked his gear—roping reins in left hand, nylon rope coiled on top, lariat tucked under right arm.

They had to beat a time of five-point-two seconds, so there could be no mistakes. They especially couldn't afford the ten-second penalty for breaking the barrier string.

A glance told him the steer was square in the chute, eyes forward.

He nodded.

The steer broke from the chute and Hank spurred his horse. The neck of his horse broke the barrier string perfectly. Rising in the stirrups, he swung his lasso. His horse caught the steer's left hip with two deep strides, hazing the animal to the right. His eyes beaded on the horns, Hank released the lariat. The loop bounced off the nose and caught on the horns. He grabbed the slack and pulled, dallying the rope around his saddle horn—thumb up, counter-clockwise—once, twice.

Hank pulled his horse to a stop, letting the animal take the brunt of the steer's jerk straight-on. As soon as the steer reached the end of the rope, he turned the horse to the left, making an L across the arena, placing the steer in position for Travis's toss.

Hank's eyes never left the steer. One stride, two. Travis

threw and caught both hind feet. As Travis dallied, Hank pulled his horse around. They faced one another, the steer stretched between them.

The field judge dropped his flag.

The crowd surged to their feet, cheering wildly.

"A perfect catch!" the announcer screamed.

A shrill whistle pierced through the applause, reminding him of Alex's whistle the day he met her at the Whiskey Mountain Café. Was this whistle hers? His eyes cut to crowd. The brief glimpse showed her jumping up and down like crazy, with two unladylike fingers in her mouth.

Hank felt warmth flow over him like sunshine. That one whistle meant more to him than all the other cheers.

Their work done, Hank and Travis eased up on the steer. As Travis's rope went slack, the steer hopped out of it. Hank headed for the holding pen with the steer, easing his rope free as the announcer got the time.

"Four point two seconds! A team roping record for Spindel rodeo! Ladies and gentlemen, the Eden brothers are in the money!"

"Did you enjoy our ride?"

Alex pulled her eyes from Claire, who was talking with several friends over by the gate. Travis approached her, stuffing his check into his shirt pocket. "I sure did. It was exciting, but over so quick."

He grinned and patted his pocket. "The quicker, the bigger the check."

She peered around him. "Where's Hank?"

"He's in there chewing the fat with Spindel. He'll be out in a minute."

She studied Travis's profile as he watched the crowd milling around the rodeo office. "You think a lot of Hank, don't you?"

Travis stood on spread legs, balancing his weight on both feet. "He's always been my hero, ever since I was little."

Alex glanced back at the office door. "He's a good choice for a hero."

"Kinda sweet on him, aren't you?" Travis asked. "He likes you, too. In fact, I've never seen him this sweet on anybody."

Alex felt her cheeks flame. "Probably all the desserts I make him."

He chuckled. "Maybe. But I think it's more than that."

She hadn't straightened out her feelings for Hank in her own mind. She certainly wasn't going to discuss them with Travis. "What about you? You don't have a woman you're sweet on?"

"Sure. Three. They're waiting for me right now."

"Where?"

He pointed towards the pens.

Alex slapped him playfully. "I didn't mean your horses."

He shrugged and his smile faded. "Life on the road is tough enough for a man alone. Hauling a family around makes it even tougher. Something always gives. Either the marriage fails or the cowboy loses his competitive edge. I've seen it happen too often." He shook his head. "Cowboys serious about making it to the National Finals don't have any business with a family."

"Don't you want a family?"

"Sure, someday. I just haven't met a woman yet who made me want to give up competition."

She placed her hand on his arm. "You will someday. And when you do, I pity the poor girl."

He raised both brows. "Am I that bad?"

She sighed dramatically. "If you're half as stubborn as your brother, she won't stand a chance."

As the last strains of the lively tune faded into the walls of the rodeo dance hall, Hank led Alex off the floor.

Her cheeks were flushed and her eyes sparkled as she lifted her face. "Dancing is fun. I should've tried it a long time ago."

Hank squeezed her waist. He could dance all night—but only with Alex. "You couldn't. You didn't have me there to teach you."

"As if someone else couldn't have taught me?"

He bent his head so his lips were next to her ear. "Not like I did."

The red on her cheeks deepened at his reminder, and she stuck a playful elbow in his ribs.

"I'm thirsty," he said. "You want a beer?"

She wrinkled her nose. "I've never acquired a taste for beer. But a soft drink would be nice."

He nodded. "I'll be back in a minute."

He was stopped so many times to relive the four-second win and for congratulatory handshakes, it was twenty minutes before he made it back to Alex with two soft drinks. His frown chased away the two cowboys flirting with her, and he handed her a drink.

"I thought you were having beer," she commented after taking a sip.

He shook his head. "Not if you don't like the taste of it."

"What does that have to— Oh."

"Darlin', you blush more than any woman I've ever seen," he said for her ears alone.

She glared at him. "Only around you."

He chuckled. Far from making him feel bad, her accusation made him feel warm deep inside. That, added to the high he'd ridden all day, had him looking down from the clouds. He'd forgotten how it felt to compete before a crowd...to win.

"Travis and Claire seem to be having fun," Alex said in an obvious attempt to change the subject.

Hank's eyes sought his brother and sister. Travis sat at a table with several other cowboys and even more women. The buckle chasers outnumbered the cowboys two to one. Claire was on the dance floor with a boy who played football for Dubois High School. She didn't look all that interested in her partner, but he knew his sister loved to dance. "Yep."

"I watched you give pointers to that bunch of boys over there," Alex said. "I could tell it meant a lot to them."

Hank shrugged. "I always take time for the little guys. I was a little guy once. I know how it felt when one of the winners took time to talk to me."

"You really love the rodeo, don't you?"

He glanced over the crowd on the dance floor. He was glad she'd noticed. "Yep."

"But this is the first time you've competed in eight years, right?"

"Yep."

"Why? Claire said there were lots of men who do it part-time. If you love it so much, why didn't you continue to compete on a regional level?"

"There are lots of reasons," he told her. "I had to bring the ranch out of debt. I had Travis and Claire to raise. Those things took all the time I had. But mostly it was because, well... There's an old saying that goes, 'If you aren't the lead steer, the view never changes.' If I couldn't have it all, I didn't want any of it. I was headed for a national championship. How could I go back to being a local yokel?"

"But you competed today, and you won. You can't tell me that doesn't feel good. I can see it all over your face."

He couldn't keep from grinning. "It felt great, just like I remembered."

"You should enter more rodeos, then."

"Yeah, well, I've been thinking about doing just that."

"You should," she said without hesitation. "You obviously love it or you wouldn't spend so much time practicing at home. And you even get paid for it. Most men can't say that about their hobbies."

Hank felt a twinge of guilt. Alex didn't understand that rodeoing was going to be more than his hobby. A few months from now it would be his full-time job. But there was no reason to tell her. She wouldn't understand why a man would voluntarily turn himself into a rambling rodeo hand. The security of home meant too much to her. Besides, he didn't want to talk about that tonight. He felt too good. He wanted to concentrate on the woman looking at him like he was the only man in the room.

The local band began a slow number. Determined to push reality away for a few more hours, Hank took Alex's half-finished drink from her hand, placed it on a nearby table beside his and led her onto the dance floor. He drew her into his arms and settled her close against him.

He rested his chin on top of her head as they swayed gently to the music—warmth against warmth, heartbeats in tune. He couldn't have Alex long, but he had her now. For the moment that was good enough.

"Alex. Darlin', we're home. Wake up."

Shaken gently from her sleep, Alex woke to find herself sprawled across the truck seat. She rose groggily to her elbow and looked around. Her eyes came to rest on Hank's dark form standing in the open door. "I fell asleep?"

"Yep. You used my shoulder for a pillow. Claire used yours."

"Why didn't you wake me?"

"I enjoyed having you snuggle against me. Even if you weren't aware of it, I sure as hell was."

Alex straightened and pushed the hair from her face. "Where's Claire?"

"She woke when we got home and went on up to bed."

"Oh. What time is it?"

"Let's see, we left Lander around midnight. It's about three, I guess."

Alex frowned and tried to shake the grogginess from her mind. "I thought the drive was just a couple of hours."

"It is. While you were snoozing, I stabled my roping horse and swept out the trailer."

"You should've wakened me."

"Then you'd have gone in and I wouldn't have collected my rain check." Hank climbed in the cab and closed the door.

Alarm made her head clear instantly. "What are you doing?"

"If you're not coming out, I'm coming in." He gathered her in his arms and bent his head toward hers.

She stopped him with a hand against his chest. "You asked before you kissed me last time."

"Are you going to make me ask every single time?"

She lifted her chin. "Maybe you'd better, so things don't get out of hand."

He sighed, then asked, "Can I kiss you, Alex?"

She shook her head with a playful smile. "Not yet."

"When? I've been dying to kiss you again all day."

Knowing he wanted her as badly as she wanted him made shivers of desire race one another across her skin. But she had to keep things light, and as calm as possible. "This was a date, right?"

"Right."

"Then we have to do things properly. This is where I tell you I had a wonderful time."

"I had a great time, too. Can I kiss you now?"

"Not yet. This is where you ask if you can call me again sometime. Although in our case, I don't know exactly what you'd say. Since there's only one phone in the house—"

He put a finger over her lips. "This is where I ask you if you'd like to go riding with me tomorrow. Maybe a picnic by the river."

"You mean a real ride? Not going round and round the corral a hundred times like I've been doing for the past week?"

"Yeah. I'd like to show you the ranch before…"

"Before I leave," she finished.

"We'll talk about that some other time."

"All right. Well then, this must be where I say 'I'd love to.'"

"Can I kiss you now?"

"Not yet. We haven't set a time. Not too early, please. As late as it is now, I'll want to sleep for a few hours at least."

Hank leaned his forehead against hers. "Woman, you're killing me. How about eleven? I've got some chores to take care of first."

"And I'll need to fix a lunch."

"How about eleven?"

"Eleven is perfect."

''Now?''

Alex slipped her arms around his neck. ''Now.''

With a growl coming from deep in his throat, his lips descended on hers.

# Chapter Eight

Several days later Hank lay stretched out on a quilt spread beneath a stand of aspens by the Wind River, his head in Alex's lap. She gently removed his hat and ran her fingers through his thick dark hair.

"Mmm, that feels good."

"I thought you were asleep."

He cracked one eye open. "Planning some hanky-panky?"

"Maybe."

One instant Alex leaned against an aspen, then next she was flat on her back, gazing up into eyes that were the same color as the sky. "Gracious!"

He grinned. "Thought I'd better keep an eye on you, just in case."

Alex slid her arms around his neck. "Is that all you're going to do?"

The cool blue eyes suddenly turned hot. "Darlin', I'll do anything you want me to, as long as you want me to do it. Just say the word."

"Anything?"

"You name it."

"Would you swim to the North Pole to get me a block of ice? Would you fly to Paris to buy me an ounce of perfume?"

"Yes."

He said it so seriously, she had to laugh. "Liar."

He shook his head. "I'd go because I know you wouldn't send me on a whim. If you had to have Arctic ice, I know it would be for a damn good reason."

She ran her fingertips over the chiseled planes of his cheek. "How do you know that?"

"I've tried to buy you things right here in Wyoming, but you refused."

"I did not need the necklace you tried to buy me in Dubois. Or the earrings."

"You didn't want them because you thought I was trying to buy my way into your...affections."

"Weren't you?"

"I just wanted to give you something to..." His eyes clouded over.

"Remem—"

"Shhh!" He winced at the harsh sound and softened his voice. He shifted to his side, one arm supporting his upper body, the other wrapped around her waist. "Don't say it."

Alex's heart performed a somersault in her chest. "You really do have a problem talking about things, don't you? Not talking about it doesn't mean it's not going to happen."

"I know. But we agreed to enjoy the time we have together. How can we enjoy it if we're constantly talking about you leaving?"

She sighed, conceding him the point. She knew she was going to pay for the intense happiness she felt today with equally intense pain, but she'd adopted Hank's philosophy wholeheartedly. She'd rather be sorry for spending this time with Hank, than be sorry for not spending it with him. His arms felt too good for her to worry about it now.

He watched his finger trace a path along her jaw. "I wish..."

"What do you wish?" she whispered, almost afraid to know.

His frown deepened. "I wish we had more time. I wish…I think you know what I wish, but we both know it can't happen."

It could, she knew, but only if she was willing to let go of her dream. Was she?

Not unless she was absolutely, positively certain that what she and Hank shared was real, would last. She didn't want a home for a few months or a few years. She'd been there, done that. She wanted something that would last the rest of her life.

Was this love that consumed her whenever she was around this man? She'd never been in love, so she didn't know. She only knew that when she was in Hank's arms, like now, she felt like she could fly to the stars. When his lips were on hers, the plan she'd thought out so carefully, been so determined to see through, seemed unimportant.

Confused, she tightened her arms around Hank's neck. "You're right. Let's don't talk about it now. Kiss me."

He lifted a brow. "Are you giving me prior approval?"

"I'm giving you an order. Please hurry."

With a deep-throated chuckle, he pressed his lips to hers. His salty-sweet taste overpowered her other senses momentarily, filling her with his flavor. She wanted to hold on to him forever.

His lips left her mouth, searing a path over to her ear. His tongue dipped inside, then he whispered, "I want to touch your breasts."

She felt her nipples tighten just at the thought. This was a new step in their relationship. Did she dare take it?

"I won't hurt you."

Alex took his hand from her waist and guided it upward. She wasn't bold enough to actually place it on her breast, but he got the message. His hand continued up and tenderly took the weight of one breast in his hand.

She gasped and called his name.

"I'm here, darlin'. You okay?"

"Oh, yes."

"Does that feel good?"

She opened her eyes to find him watching her face intently. "Yes."

"Damn! It feels good to me, too."

He ran his thumb across her nipple. Her body tried to jump out of its skin.

He lowered his head to her chest. His hot breath covered one peak. Her hips ground up against the leg he'd laid over them.

He groaned loudly and his teeth plucked at the top button of her blouse. "I want to taste you."

She wanted his lips on hers, too. She tried to pull his head up so their lips could meet.

His head lifted, but instead of kissing her, he looked down with eyes that scorched every place they touched. "Can I get rid of your shirt and bra?"

Her skin tingled all over in anticipation of his hot mouth sliding over her, everywhere. Her hands ached with the longing to rip her blouse open and bare herself like a sacrifice, but instead she curled them into fists.

Tears of frustration stung her eyes. "I don't think that's a good idea."

He froze. "Do you think I'm going to hurt you?"

She shook her head.

"Do you think that once I get you undressed, I won't stop?"

Her eyes fell to his throat. "Maybe."

He forced her chin up. "You don't trust me."

She swallowed miserably. "I don't trust myself. If we make love, I don't think I'll be able to leave."

Hank's eyes burned into hers for a long moment. "I could tell you I'd stop before we went that far, but I'm not sure I could."

"I'm sorry," she said quietly.

"No." He placed a finger over her lips. "You don't have anything to be sorry for. You're right."

"I know you're frustrated."

"And you're not?"

She smiled. "You mean you can't tell?"

His eyes drifted down her body, lingering on her swollen lips and tight nipples she was certain showed through her blouse.

He groaned, then suddenly stood and reached a hand for hers.

She let him draw her to her feet. "What is it?"

"I'm leading us away from temptation." He bent to place a quick kiss on her lips. "You pack up the picnic basket. I'll get the horses."

Hank was halfway up the stairs when he heard Claire's door open. Two seconds later, Alex appeared on the landing.

When she saw him, she started. "I thought you were gone."

He shook his head and continued up the stairs. "I got my horse saddled, then remembered I had to make a phone call." When he came even with Alex, he noticed her frown. "What's wrong?"

"Claire's not going to school. She's—" Alex glanced at Claire's door and lowered her voice. "She has cramps so bad she can't get out of bed."

"Okay." He leaned forward to give her a kiss.

She jerked back. "I can't believe you're being so callous. She needs to see a doctor, Hank. Soon."

His brow furrowed. "What do you mean? She's like this every month. That's not normal?"

His concern must've been evident because she relaxed her combative stance. "Of course it's not normal. Not cramps this bad."

"Yours aren't?"

Her cheeks reddened at the intimate subject, but she didn't back down. "They're uncomfortable, but not incapacitating. Don't you know anything about women's problems?"

He frowned. "Not really. I've never really been around women. I mean, I've been around women, but not day in and day out, except for Claire."

"The other cooks weren't concerned?"

"Claire hasn't been this bad except the past year. The last

cook, Mrs. Johnson, thought she was faking to get out of school.''

"Yeah, right. Claire's having so much fun in there. If Mrs. Johnson were here, I'd give her a piece of my mind.''

Hank ran a hand back through his hair. ''It's my fault. I should've paid closer attention. But Claire didn't say she needed to see a doctor.''

"Claire doesn't know what's normal any more than you do, Hank. She's still a girl in many ways. She's never had a woman around interested in her enough to teach her how to be one.''

He lifted a hand to her cheek. ''Until now.''

Alex's breath caught, and she stared up at him. In that endless moment Hank knew this was more than a physical attraction. He needed this woman as much as he wanted her—and he wanted her so bad it kept him awake at night. In the few short weeks she'd been at the Garden, she'd turned this old house into a home and the Edens into a family.

How could he let her go?

Suddenly Alex spun away from him.

Reflex made him catch her arm. ''Where are you going?''

She refused to look at him. ''Downstairs to get the heating pad and some aspirin for Claire.''

"Alex, look at me.''

His quiet voice compelled her to turn. Her eyes held misery and confusion and regret.

A band of steel tightened around Hank's chest, making it difficult to breathe. He didn't have a choice. He had to let her go—for her sake as well as his.

"Thanks for caring.'' He released her and turned. Knocking softly on Claire's door, he pushed it open and went inside.

"Now I had me a horse once that used every trick in the horse book to get out of work,'' Jed told the small group gathered on the porch. ''When I'd sashay into the corral with a bridle in my hand, he'd run away or walk away or skip away or jump away. He tried to hide in a corner or behind another horse. He'd stamp and snort and buck. When I finally did catch him, he'd hold his head so high I needed a stepladder just to set the bit.''

Alex chuckled at the description and wrapped her jacket closer around her. The temperature would dip well below freezing tonight, even though it was nearly April. But the three ranch hands were keeping the air on the back porch warm by expending a lot of hot air—their favorite evening pastime.

"Hell, that ain't nothing," Buck said. "I once had a mare so stupid, she thought she could hide behind a tree. When I went to the pasture to call her, she ran over to this scrawny little pine tree and hid her head. There'd be this skinny tree, a horse nose sticking out one side and a huge horse body sticking out the other. I reckon she thought if she couldn't see me, I couldn't see her.''

"Hey, boss," Derek said suddenly. "Everything shaping up for the trail drive Thursday?"

All eyes turned to the screen door.

Hank stood as a silhouette against the light. He pushed the door open and settled beside Alex on the swing. He drew her against his side casually, as if he'd been doing it for years. "Things are coming along. I've done all I can do tonight. Did you and Jed get that tack mended?"

That led the discussion away from the stupidity of horses to the trail drive that was still three days away, which led to reminiscences of past trail drives.

Warmth stole over Alex as she listened to the men talk, and the heat didn't all come from the man pressed against her. It came from the family that surrounded her. Even though these ranch hands weren't related to the Edens, Hank treated each one like a brother. And though Hank certainly didn't treat Alex like a sister, this extended family had opened up enough to include her.

To communicate her gratitude to the man responsible, Alex slipped a hand onto Hank's jeans-clad thigh and gave a gentle squeeze as he answered a question Buck asked.

Hank cut off his thought in mid-sentence. He turned his head just a shade more toward her and flexed his arm to draw her a hair closer. Then he went on talking as if nothing happened. The men probably saw no difference in their position, but Alex felt the subtle changes.

Emotion washed over her like a tidal wave. She felt like she'd been swept away, but at the same time felt like she was cradled in warm water. Either way, she was unable to breathe.

She loved Hank. The certainty was so strong, it made her head swim. She wanted to wrap her arms around this man—her man—and never let go. She wanted to crawl inside of him so he could keep her safe and warm. She wanted to grant his every wish, feed his every hunger, satisfy his every desire.

She wanted to tell him her feelings, to stand up and blurt it out so the whole world could hear. *Alex Miller loves Hank Eden!*

She shuddered with the power of the emotion.

"You're cold," Hank said immediately.

Cold? Not in any sense of the word.

"We need to turn in, anyway," Jed said, rising from his seat on the steps.

The three hands said good-night, then ambled toward the bunkhouse.

Hank helped Alex rise, then held the door open for her. She hung her jacket on a hook and turned to find him watching her. Their gazes locked, hungry, searching. Tension stretched between them like newly strung barbwire. Alex took a tiny step, then another, then she was in his arms. They felt like heaven. They felt like home.

Their kiss rocked Alex to the soles of her feet. It was as if light flowed from Hank's lips, searching out the darkest corners of her being, until her whole body glowed.

His hands spread over her back, pulling her so close she couldn't tell whose heartbeat was whose. But it didn't matter. Their hearts beat together.

"Damn," he gasped when they finally came up for air. "Not that I'm complaining, but what was that for?"

She pushed her hands back through his thick, close-cropped hair. "For being you."

"Hell, I'm me every day. But you haven't kissed me like that before."

This was her opportunity. All she had to say were three small, common words. *I love you.*

She opened her mouth, but instead of speaking, she pulled his head back down and kissed him again.

What if he didn't feel the same? What if he didn't want her to stay at the Garden? Now that she thought about it, Hank had never asked her to stay. Claire asked, all the ranch hands asked, Hen all but demanded she stay last time Alex talked to her. But Hank never did.

Dread crept through her, and all the reasons she hadn't wanted to go out with Hank in the first place flashed across her mind.

Maybe he was just being noble, because he thought she still wanted to study under Monsieur Buchaude. And she did. Didn't she?

The trouble was, she didn't know what she wanted.

No, that wasn't true. She knew exactly what she wanted. She wanted both Hank and the opportunity in California. But she couldn't have both. She had to risk one or the other.

Tears of frustration stung her eyes. To drive them away, she pulled Hank closer, knowing his kisses would make her forget there was any choice but his arms.

The phone rang shrilly, disturbing the comfortable silence in the parlor and pulling Hank's mind from the article on D-ring bits.

"You want me to get it?" Alex asked lazily from the crook of his arm.

He placed a soft kiss on her forehead. "That's okay. I'll get up."

He disentangled himself from her arms and caught the phone in the kitchen on the fourth ring. "Hello?"

"Mr. Eden? This is Dennis Cowden, Ranch Realty."

Hank reached over and closed the kitchen door. "Yes?"

"Sorry about calling so late, but I just got back in the office. Had to drive up to Mule Creek Junction today to look at some property. When I got back, I had a packet on my desk I knew you'd want to hear about."

"Another offer?"

"Not just another offer, Mr. Eden. *The* offer." The agent quoted a sum that made Hank lean against the counter for support.

"Who's it from?" Hank asked when the agent paused for breath laying out the details.

"Some Japanese corporation. I'm not gonna pretend I know how to pronounce it," the agent replied. "So, what do you think?"

"Japanese? They're going to develop it?"

"Hell, I don't know what they're going to do. What does it matter? With this much money, you could buy a spread three times the one you've got in any other part of the state."

Hank ran a hand back through his hair. "How long do I have to think about it?"

"Well, they want to take possession by June first, so I wouldn't take more than a week. The paperwork's gonna take at least six weeks."

"June first? Then they are going to develop it. To get anything built around here, construction has to start at the beginning of the summer."

"June first a problem?"

All Hank had to do was say Okay, and he'd be free. The Japanese corporation wanted the ranch "lock, stock and barrel" which meant all he had to do was walk away. He didn't even have to sell the cattle.

No more worrying about falling beef prices. No more late nights pulling calves. He'd be back on the rodeo circuit in time for the busiest rodeo season of the year.

He glanced out the window at the barn, lit by a strong floodlight, the barn built by his grandfather. If Hank said okay, the only home he'd ever known would cease to exist in two months. "I'll get back to you."

"You aren't thinking about pulling out now, are you?" the agent asked.

"I still can, can't I?"

There was a brief silence on the other end of the line.

"Well, if you can afford to turn your back on this much money, sure. But you'd be a damn fool."

Hank's face tightened. "I have to discuss the offer with my brother and sister. They're in on this decision, too."

"Okay, sure. Whatever. Give me a call. Just don't wait too long. They might find some other property they like better."

Hank hung up the phone, then opened the kitchen door and stepped onto the back porch. A full moon hung over the tips of the mountains, making a jagged silhouette against the light.

So, the time had come to decide. He hadn't thought this moment would come for at least a couple of months. What the hell was he going to do? A month ago, it had all seemed so easy, so clear. Getting back to the rodeo was worth any price. Now things weren't so simple.

"You okay?"

He turned to see Alex standing quietly in the door. "Yeah."

She stepped onto the porch, and he drew her into his arms.

"It wasn't bad news, was it?" she asked.

He shook his head. "I just needed some fresh air."

She relaxed against him. Having Alex in his arms made him feel warm, content, whole. What could the rodeo give him that could compare to this? Sure, winning felt good, but that only lasted a few seconds a day. And he wouldn't always win. With Alex, he felt like a winner every time he touched her. If only he could ask her to stay here at the Garden forever.

Misery washed over him. Damned or damned.

If he turned down the offer he was fairly certain he could persuade Alex to stay, but for how long? Would she stick by him when he lost the home she wanted so badly? If he accepted the Japanese offer, she'd leave. He couldn't ask her to share the rambling life of a rodeo cowboy.

Hank pulled away enough to lift her chin. "Kiss?"

She slipped her arms around his neck. "I'm sorry I ever insisted you ask. From now on you have blanket permission for everything up to and including kissing. Now, please…"

He wrapped himself around her and pulled her close, losing himself in the feel, the smell, the taste of his woman. He still had a few more days to put off his decision. The trail drive would take up the next two days, then he had to get in touch with Travis.

Yes, he was damned. But not tonight. Tonight she was here, she was his. There was nothing else in the world that mattered.

"Ready to mount? The men already have the herd moving."

Alex glanced over her shoulder. In the early-morning twilight, she saw Hank pulling three horses by the reins. "Almost. Just checking to make sure I didn't forget anything. There isn't a store I can run to where we're going."

"Take your time. They're going slow. We'll catch up easily."

He waited patiently while she double-checked the contents of the two bags. They held the ingredients and utensils for the meals she would cook for the crew driving the Eden herd to their spring pastures.

Finally she stood and dusted off her hands. "I guess I'm ready. I've never done this before. I hope I can fix something edible for so many people on an open fire."

Hank snaked his free hand around her waist. "You haven't disappointed us yet."

She smiled at him wryly. "Yes, well, I've been working on a stove. I just turn a knob and 'Poof' I have nice, even heat."

Hank leaned down and pressed a light kiss on her mouth. As he pulled away, she moaned so softly he didn't hear. He handed her the reins of all three horses, then bent to load one of the bags onto the one that wasn't saddled.

The dim light and the jacket he wore against the early-morning chill hid Hank's muscled back. But as he lifted and tied the heavy sack, she didn't need to see in order to imagine those muscles flexing. She knew each one by heart, knew how each one moved under her hands as she held him, as he held her.

Alex moaned again.

"You say something?" he asked as he bent to lift the other sack.

She shook her head.

She was sorely tempted to give Hank permission for intimacies far beyond kissing. The last few nights, when he held her close and kissed her good-night, she didn't want the night to end there. She wanted more. She wanted him, and everything that went with him.

When the bay mare named Julie nudged her arm, Alex stroked her nose absently.

But Hank still hadn't asked her to stay. There were times when it seemed like he wanted to ask. She could actually see him struggling with himself. But he never said the words.

Which was just as well, since she still didn't know which she would choose. Her time was just about up. She only had five more days to decide. That's when her month's employment at the Garden officially ended.

"Where's our bedrolls?" he asked when he finished loading the supplies.

Alex pointed to the porch. "On the swing."

He took the steps two at a time and retrieved two canvas rolls wrapped around foam pads, wool blankets, sheets and clothes. He didn't ask which one was his, just tied one behind each saddle. Then he unlooped the lead on the pack horse and tied it to a ring on the back of Julie's saddle. The pack horse would be Alex's responsibility during the drive.

His eyes roamed over their gear as he made his way around Julie. Finally he faced her. "Ready?"

Alex took one last look at the house. Even through the dim light, she saw movement in her bedroom window.

Sugar. Tonight would be the first time they slept apart since she found him four years ago.

Hank's arm curled around her waist, and he pulled her against his side. "The house will get along without you for one night."

She looked at him, startled. She didn't realize he'd noticed how much she loved the old house that had come alive under her care. Of course she would miss it. Though she knew it wasn't the smartest thing to do, she'd already begun to think of it as home.

She ran a hand over the bristle on Hank's face. He hadn't

shaved that morning. She stretched up on her toes and kissed him. "I'm ready."

She guided the split reins back over Julie's head, then crossed them over the saddle horn. With her knee against her chest, she placed her left toe into the stirrup. As she hopped, preparing to spring into the saddle, she felt two strong hands circle her waist and half lift her into it. "I wish that just once, you'd let me mount by myself. How do you know if I'm even able to?"

Hank ducked under Julie's nose, grabbed the reins of his own horse, then sprang easily into the saddle. "There'll be enough men around to help if you have to remount."

"What if there aren't?"

"There will be. If there aren't, I'll have somebody's hide." With that, he turned his horse away from the house.

Alex sighed audibly. At times like these she agreed with Claire—cowboys could use a little less testosterone. She wasn't about to tell Hank she'd been practicing on her own, during the day when he wasn't there. For her own peace of mind, she had to be certain she could saddle, mount, dismount and unsaddle a horse all by herself. Let him think she was a frail flower. Most of the time she liked the way he treated her. His tender care was something she could definitely get used to.

Hank's weary feet found the worn path by rote. Eden cattle drives had camped at this spot for nearly a hundred years. Two-thirds of the way to the spring pastures, it was the perfect spot, with a year-round creek running through a plateau surrounded by pines. He knew it as well as he knew the creases in his boots.

Ahead, the dull glow of the campfire beckoned. He was the last cowboy on the first guard to head in. He didn't need a watch to tell him it was several hours after midnight. Casey, one of the married hands, and Jed probably beat him to bed by at least half an hour. He was looking forward to his own bedroll. It had been a tiring day.

Hank's long strides quickly brought him to the low circle

of light surrounding the campfire. He wasn't surprised to see it built up. Casey or Jed would've taken care of that before turning in.

Against the circle of logs surrounding the area—felled decades ago to act as both benches and heat trap—lay an assortment of bodies wrapped in blankets. Which one was Alex?

Then he spied her, and a curse tore from his throat. Instead of being cozily snuggled in her bedroll, she leaned against a log on the opposite side of the fire, fast asleep, chin on her chest.

He started around the fire, then saw a pot still on the grate over the flames. Grabbing the tongs on one rock supporting the grate, he pulled the pot off the fire. It felt half full. She'd evidently stayed up to make coffee for the second watch, then waited for him.

She was shivering in the night air, and he saw her tighten her arms around her body. He was going to give her hell in the morning, but for now he had to get her warm.

Their tightly wrapped bedrolls lay beside her. He unbuckled the leather belts keeping them together and laid them side by side between the log and the fire. On second thought, he rearranged the sheets and blankets to make one big bed instead of two smaller ones. They'd both get warm faster if they shared body heat. She'd probably shoot him in the morning, but he'd worry about it then. They couldn't do anything, anyway, with so many people around. He just wanted to hold her.

His task done, he bent down and lifted her in his arms.

She startled awake with a gasp. Her eyes searched wildly until they fell on him. She relaxed and smiled sleepily. "Hank."

"Why aren't you in bed?"

She yawned and stretched. "Hmm?"

"You should've been in bed hours ago. The hands can make their own damn coffee."

"I just—" she yawned again "—wanted to see you." Her head lolled against his shoulder. She rubbed her cheek against the rough denim of his jacket and snuggled deeper into his arms.

Emotion stampeded through Hank as he knelt on the blankets and laid her down gently.

She just wanted to see him.

He was glad she was asleep. If she'd been awake, there's no way he'd be able to yell at her for nearly freezing to death. He'd be too busy kissing her.

He pulled off her jacket and tugged off her boots, then settled her between the blankets. After performing the same services for himself, he slid in beside her. He pushed a strand of hair off her cheek, then placed a kiss on it.

"You're the damnedest woman I've ever known. What the hell am I going to do with you? Or without you?"

# Chapter Nine

Alex snuggled deeper into the warmth. It couldn't possibly be time to get up. Dimly aware of movement around the campfire, she turned on her side away from the fire and hit her nose on a hard, unmoving wall.

Surprise cleared her head and she instinctively pulled back. Her eyes popped open, but she could only see a dark shape close beside her. Hank. She would know him if she were blind—by his smell and the warmth of his arms.

So what woke her? The tales of grizzly bears that had kept her awake, waiting for Hank, spun through her head. Moving slowly, she peered over her shoulder, then relaxed. Just Casey building up the fire.

The arm Hank had draped over her eased around to her back, bringing her attention to the man in her arms. She whispered, "Are you awake?"

He leaned forward to place a kiss on her temple. "No."

"What are you doing in my bedroll?" she asked quietly.

"When I came in from my watch last night, you were shivering *beside* it." He brushed a strand of hair from her face. "Remind me later to give you a lecture on the dangers of hypothermia."

She shuddered and crept a little closer. "I couldn't go to sleep. Derek and Buck told me about the grizzly bears that roam the mountains. I wanted to keep the fire going and...and..."

"And what?"

"And wait for you," she said, glad the darkness hid her hot cheeks.

"So I could keep the monsters away?" he asked softly.

Alex buried her head under his chin and moaned. "That sounds childish, doesn't it? I wasn't thinking about it that way. I just..."

"Yes?"

"I just feel safer when you're around."

He gathered her closer and lifted her mouth for his kiss— warm, deep.

When he pulled away, she sighed. "I suppose I should get up and start breakfast. It's near dawn, isn't it?"

"Another hour, probably."

"You said last night you need to have the herd moving by first light."

"Yep."

"Then..." She tried to sit up, but he held her down.

"Just a few more minutes," he breathed.

Alex glanced over her shoulder. "What will your men think when they see us sleeping together?"

"Who cares?"

"Hank, please..."

He peered around her at the fire. "Casey's the only one awake. He won't say anything. And we'll be up before the others, I swear." He drew her closer. "Please, Alex. I don't wake up with a beautiful woman in my arms every day. I want to enjoy it."

Alex sighed and sank into him. How could she argue with that?

Reaching the outcropping perched above Eden Valley, Hank reined in and for the first time all day, took a moment to look beyond the herd. The sun had climbed high overhead as they drove the cattle ever upward to this rich, wide valley nestled between two mountains. Though it lay on public land, the valley had been feeding Eden cattle for nearly a hundred years. Hank's great-grandfather had simply driven his cattle up the mountain. Hank now leased it. Sometime between then and now, it had been named after his family.

The herd stretched out beneath him, an undulating sea of black Angus cattle. The grass they'd already begun to eat was knee-high and green, watered by snow melt and a creek running through the middle. It would last the herd about a month, when they would have to be driven higher to grass just now beginning to green.

This was a good herd, one of the best he'd had in years. The winter hadn't been too harsh, and he'd only lost a few calves to freezing temperatures or predators.

Suddenly the words he was using penetrated. Best herd *he'd* had. *He'd* only lost a few calves.

Hank had never thought of the herd as his before. For that matter, he never thought of the ranch as his. It had always been his father's land, his father's herd, his father's house. He'd just been a caretaker, biding his time until he could leave. Until now.

Regret hit him like a punch in the gut. He would never be bringing a herd to Eden Valley again. This land had been used by his family for nearly a hundred years—and he was the one losing it.

Hank's fist tightened on the reins, and his horse shied beneath him. He pulled the bay gelding back around, then scanned the valley again.

He wished he could keep it, not only for himself and his children, but for Alex. She was the one who'd made this ranch his home, by trying to make it hers, by loving him.

For the first time in his life, he could see himself growing old at the Garden. He could see bringing his sons to Eden Valley, and his grandsons...and daughters. He closed his eyes to savor the image of lifting a small golden-eyed girl up on a horse for the first time, when he remembered the rodeo.

Hank swept off his hat and raked a hand through his hair.

What about his dreams of becoming a gold buckle hero? Was he willing to give them up, when he was so close to having another go at them?

He thought about the rodeo and the carefree life he'd had as a young man. But he wasn't young any longer, not for a rodeo cowboy. He only had a few good years left to rodeo, at best.

How could those few short years compare with having Alex for a lifetime? How could sleeping in a different cheap motel room every night compare with coming home to the ranch that had housed Edens for a hundred years?

He suddenly realized that his dreams had changed. He only needed to be a hero to one person—Alex. He could always rodeo in the local circuit....

Reality hit like a summer thunderstorm. What the hell was he thinking? He couldn't keep the Garden. He'd been trying to figure out a way to hold on for the past three years, with no success.

How could he let Alex give up her dream, when he knew he was about to lose the home she wanted—needed—so badly?

He couldn't. She deserved a better life than he could give her—nomads on the rodeo circuit.

The loss stabbed deep as his gaze swept the herd again. He hadn't known what he really wanted until it was too late. Until he was about to lose it.

Pushing the dismal thoughts away, he straightened in the saddle and searched the perimeter of the herd for his men. They were spaced out evenly, waiting for his signal to ride in. The cattle had been spread across the valley and had already settled down after their uphill journey.

To his left, Hank saw a column of smoke rising from the chimney of a small log cabin built before he was born. Alex was cooking one last meal before they headed down the mountain. Casey and his wife, Lila, would stay to watch over the herd until they were relieved by Jed and Derek in a week.

Raising his arm, Hank gave the signal for his men to ride in, then reined toward the cabin.

He spurred his mount into a gallop. He and Alex had ridden at opposite ends of the herd during the drive—he at point and she at the rear, riding drag. He intended on spending every minute possible with her on the way back.

Casey and Buck watched him ride up as they loosened the cinches on their horses.

"You sure are in a hurry, boss," Buck said.

Casey chuckled. "Yeah. You must be hungry."

"Question is, you hungry for the cook or her cookin'?" Buck slapped his knee.

Hank dismounted, unperturbed by the ribbing. He'd done a fair amount of it himself last year when Casey was smitten. "Lunch about ready?"

"Hell, I hope so," Buck said. "I could eat a whole steer."

Their heads turned as one when the cabin door opened. Alex came out onto the porch. "You boys ready to eat?"

Hank bounded up the four steps to the porch and took Alex in his arms. He didn't give her time to protest as he kissed her hard and deep, ignoring the whistles and comments from their audience.

"What was that for?" she gasped, when his lips finally released hers.

"To thank you."

"For what?"

He couldn't keep the sadness from his smile. "For being you."

She frowned. "Hank, are you—"

"What's going on, Derek?"

Jed's call brought everyone's attention to the tall cowboy. Hank glanced around. Derek hadn't dismounted at the cabin but instead had guided his horse to the south side. The hand's attention was somewhere down the trail.

Hank pulled Alex to the edge of the porch. "What do you see?"

"Someone's coming up the trail, boss," Derek told him.

Relieved that Derek's eagle-sharp eyes hadn't spotted some kind of predator bearing down on the herd, he called, "Can you make out who it is?"

The hand shook his head. "They're riding the cherry roan mare from the Garden. Must be Claire.... Yep, it is. She's riding like devil's after her." Derek spurred his horse and rode out to meet her.

Hank hopped the porch rail and strode over to the spot Derek had just left. "What the hell..."

"She wasn't supposed to come with us, was she, boss?" Jed asked from right behind him.

"She had a test yesterday in English that she couldn't miss," Alex told him as she came up and slipped her hand into Hank's.

"You think something happened to the Garden?" Casey asked.

"Of course something's happened," Buck said. "Claire wouldn't come racing up here for nothing."

"Whatever's happened, we know Claire is okay," Alex said.

Hank squeezed her hand gratefully.

"Maybe a barn burned down," Buck said.

"Or the house," Casey added.

Hank threw a glance around the group. "We'll know soon enough."

The group became so quiet, he could hear the two horses' pounding hooves get louder and louder.

Finally Derek topped the hill. Claire was a length behind. In another three strides, she reined in the foam-flecked roan. "Hank, it's Travis."

Hank grabbed her bridle, his heart slamming to a stop. All the rodeo injuries he'd seen over the years raced across his mind—from being gored by a bull to necks broken by falls from broncs. "What happened?"

Claire's wide, frightened eyes filled with tears. "He's in the hospital in Phoenix. The doctor called this morning. He hasn't—" she released a small sob "—hasn't woken up yet."

"Bull riding?"

She nodded. "The bull came after him when he got off. His ribs, his arm, his head. I can't remember what all the doctor said. But they want us to come."

"As soon as we get fresh mounts." He turned and searched the group. "I'll take the gelding Lila was riding. Casey, give Claire Alex's mare. Alex and Lila can take the roan and the bay."

"Right, boss."

Jed headed for the bay Hank rode in. "I'll switch saddles for you."

Buck moved to help Casey with the other horses. Derek dismounted and helped Claire down from the roan.

"I'll get something for you to eat." Lila turned toward the cabin.

Alex put a hand on Hank's arm. "Do you want me to come with you?"

He shook his head. "We'll be riding too fast for too long. You'd just slow us down. The others will be heading back this afternoon. Ride with them. You should be home by nightfall."

Casey led the gelding up then and handed Hank the reins. Hank kissed Alex on the forehead, looking like his mind was a thousand miles away, then mounted. Claire urged her horse beside his, and they conversed softly for a moment.

Her eyes stinging with tears she refused to let fall, Alex backed away. Suddenly all the things Hank hadn't said took on new meaning.

He didn't want her to go with him.

She knew she had no right to feel this way, but she couldn't stop the stab of desolation that swept through her. She wasn't an Eden. She'd tried to make herself part of this family, but when family really mattered, Hank and Claire were riding off without her. The pain was achingly familiar—deserted again. Yet another place where she didn't belong.

Unable to breathe, she turned to escape into the cabin.

"Alex!"

His bellow stopped her in her tracks.

"Where the hell are you going?"

She turned slowly to see the hands parting to let Hank's horse through. Her heart hammered at the look on his face. When he reached her, he leaned over, grabbed her under her arms and pulled her up in front of him. Burying his face in her neck, he breathed, "Why were you running away?"

She held on with all her strength. "You were leaving me."

He pulled back so he could see her face, his own clearly confused. "Darlin', you wouldn't be able to keep up with us. I want you to go, but—" Suddenly he looked down, then behind him.

Looking over his shoulder, Alex saw everyone staring at them.

"Don't you people have something else to do?" Hank scowled.

They turned their heads toward Claire, who suddenly found her watch fascinating.

"You need to get going," Alex told him softly.

"But I need to explain why—"

She shook her head. "You already did. And Travis needs you. I'm okay now. It was just an old childish bugaboo of mine, being left behind." She smiled as trembling fingers traced his unshaven jaw. "You chased my monster away."

His brows furrowed. "I did? How?"

"By making me feel like you need me."

He searched the depths of her eyes before uttering, "God forgive me, I do need you."

Her heart hammering with love and excitement, she leaned forward and kissed him. They weren't exactly the words she wanted to hear, but they were close enough. "You'd better go."

He kissed her once more, then set her down. "We'll be gone by the time you get home. I'll call from the hospital."

She nodded. "I'll wait up."

He shook his head and turned the gelding around. "Get some sleep. I won't call till morning."

"You'll be flying?"

"No. There's not a plane out of Jackson until tomorrow. We can be there by then."

"Be careful," she called as he and Claire rode away. Then she added softly, "I love you."

* * *

Alex ran down the hall and grabbed the phone on the second ring. "Hello? Hank?"

"He's okay" were the first words Hank uttered.

"Thank goodness!" She sank to the floor in relief. "He's awake, then?"

"Yep. Came to last night. Can't get much out of him, though. They've given him enough painkillers to kill a moose. He's trussed up like a branded calf and keeps mumbling something about Japan. Maybe he's dreaming about geisha girls."

"What's wrong with him?"

"Concussion, cracked ribs, multiple arm fractures, dislocated shoulder. You name it."

"When are you bringing him home?"

"Can't leave until tomorrow. The doc wants to keep him under observation at least twenty-four hours, make sure his brains aren't scrambled. I told the doc they already were."

"Hank..."

He sighed wearily over the line. "Damn, I miss you."

"I miss you, too. The house seems empty with nobody here but me and Sugar. What time did you get in?"

"Around dawn."

"You probably haven't slept at all, have you?"

"No. Have you?"

"I tried." She stroked Sugar's head as he jumped on her lap. "Long-distance is expensive. Be careful driving back. When should I expect you?"

"Not till late. We'll have to drive through because of Travis's horses."

"Okay. I'll keep something warm. Get some sleep, okay? You've got a long drive tomorrow."

"Okay. Bye, darlin'. See you soon."

"Hurry home."

The line clicked off and Alex stared at the receiver. In that instant she knew without a doubt that the Garden was her home. She didn't want a restaurant anymore. How could customers be her family? She had a family right here who needed her, who wanted her as much as she wanted them.

Grinning, she wrapped her arms around Sugar and squeezed, tears of happiness spilling onto his orange fur.

Alex woke with a start, sending the book on her chest sliding to the floor. The loud thump helped clear her brain. Over the barking of dogs she could hear the low rumble of trucks coming up the drive.

Hank was home.

She jumped up and ran down the hall. A quick glance at the grandfather clock told her it was nearly midnight. She skidded to a halt at the mud room. Though her first instinct was to run outside and throw herself into Hank's arms, she probably should check on their supper. The last time she remembered doing it was around ten.

As she stirred the soup and turned up the heat, she heard one truck head into the garage. The other stopped at the barn.

Dropping the lid into place, she hurried outside to find Hank walking stiffly across the yard to Travis's rig. He stopped for a moment when he saw her. Since he looked like he couldn't decide between coming to her or continuing to the barn, she took the decision away. Running down the steps, she raced across the yard to be enfolded in his arms. Their lips met in a hungry dance, then he buried his face in her hair.

"Thank goodness you're home," she breathed.

He kissed her again, deeply, then turned her in his arms so they could walk to Travis's rig. "You were worried?"

"You're so late."

"Checking him out took the whole damn morning. It was close to noon before we left the hospital."

Claire came around the front of Travis's truck as they approached.

"How's he doing?" Hank called.

"About the same," she answered. "You'd better help me open the door. He's been asleep. He may fall out."

The cab door opened, and a deep, scratchy voice uttered, "I can do it."

As the door swung open, Travis tumbled out, his good arm

scrambling for purchase. Hank caught him just before he fell face-down in the dirt.

Travis cussed and shoved away from his brother. "I said I can do it." He stumbled back a few steps, then squinted around at them. His eyes finally fell on the house.

Alex held her breath. This man didn't look or act like the same Travis she'd met a few weeks before. His angular, handsome face was swollen, the entire left side dark with bruises. His left arm was in a sling, cradled against his ribs.

"He sounds drunk," Alex whispered to Claire.

"It's the medicine." Claire closed the truck door as Travis lurched across the drive. Hank followed. "He slept most of the way, thank Heaven. I might have killed him if he hadn't."

"He must be in a lot of pain," Alex noted.

Claire harrumphed.

"You want me to help unload the horses?"

She shook her head. "I can handle it. Why don't you see if Mr. Personality will let you help him to bed? Travis won't let Hank touch him, and if I spend one more minute in his company, I'll probably—"

"All right." Alex started across the yard, calling back, "In case you get in before I come down, there's soup on the stove."

"Sounds great!" Claire called back. "I'm starving. Hank set a grueling pace that even I had trouble keeping up with. The only time I got anything to eat was when we stopped for gas. See if you can get some soup down Travis, will you? He refused everything I offered him."

"I'll try." Alex turned and sprinted across the yard. Just as she reached the porch, Travis began to teeter off the second step. Hank grabbed him from behind. The tirade Travis heaped upon his brother's head as he jerked away was only half-coherent, but the parts Alex could understand were all curses.

Hurrying forward, she slipped under Travis's arm. He tried to pull away, but she grabbed his belt and hung on. "Where you going, cowboy?"

He looked down at her, his eyes trying to focus. "Alex?"

"That's me. Where we going?"

Travis fixed his eyes on the screen door. "I'm going into *my home*. The house my great-granddaddy built near a hundred years ago." He waved at the house expansively, his speech slurred. "The house he passed down to his son, who passed it to his son, then his son, then—"

"I get the picture. But we won't get there unless we walk. There's three more steps to go, okay? That's right. Good. One more."

Hank followed them all the way upstairs, not uttering a word. Travis seemed oblivious of his presence, even during the several times Hank had to catch him as he staggered back off the stairs to the second floor. As they slowly climbed toward his bedroom, Travis kept up a broken stream of disjointed memories in the rooms they lurched through.

Finally, he fell onto his bed. He bellowed once and grabbed his rib cage. Slowly his features softened from a grimace as sleep claimed him.

Alex leaned over and pulled off his hat.

"Sorry about all this," Hank began.

Alex waved him quiet. "You're the one he's abusing, not me."

Hank removed his own hat and raked tight fingers through his hair. "I don't understand it. The last time we saw each other was at the rodeo. We got along better than we ever have. But he howled every time I walked into his hospital room, like I was punching him in the ribs."

Hank pulled her close and kissed her with a fervency that set her blood boiling, then he walked her to the door. "I heard you tell Claire you've got some soup on the stove. Why don't you go dish it up, while I get Travis out of his clothes? It shouldn't take long, now that he's asleep."

Alex started to argue, then changed her mind. Hank seemed determined to take care of his brother, whether Travis wanted him to or not. She'd better let Hank do what he could while Travis was in no shape to argue. "Don't be long."

"I won't," he promised with another kiss.

Half an hour later Alex came upstairs to see what was keeping Hank. She found him stretched across his own bed with his boots still on. Shaking her head, she pulled off his boots and covered him with a blanket.

She bent over the bed to kiss his cheek, rough from four days growth of beard. "Sweet dreams, cowboy."

Alex closed the door to the refrigerator. As the loud thump died away, she heard creaking on the stairs.

"Travis?"

She dropped two large packages of beef chuck into the sink and stepped into the hall.

"Where's Hank?" he demanded before she could say anything.

"You shouldn't be down here. What if you fell down the stairs? Go—"

"I'm tired of being treated like a kid!" he shouted.

By closing her eyes and counting to five, Alex refrained from informing him that he was treated like a kid because he acted like one. His temper sure hadn't improved since she'd taken breakfast up to him. "I'm not treating you like a kid," she said with more patience than she felt. "I'm treating you like an injured man whose mind is clouded with painkillers."

"Not today," he said grimly.

She placed her hands on her hips. "You didn't take those pills I put on your tray?"

His bruised, swollen chin rose a notch, and he steadied himself with a hand on the banister. "I flushed every damn one of them down the john."

"What's going on?" Claire asked from the head of the stairs, still in her nightgown. "Oh. Grumpy's up."

"He just told me he threw away all the painkillers the doctor prescribed."

Claire descended to the stair above Travis. "You did what? Why?"

"I'm home now. I don't need them."

"You idiot," Claire shot at him.

Alex threw up her hands. "Fine. Suffer."

"Where's Hank?" Travis demanded.

"He's working," Alex said. "Where else would he be? He

left this morning even before I was up. Jed said he went to check on the herd. Hank was dead tired last night, but he lost two days going to get you."

Claire nodded. "Hank would get out of the grave to check on the herd."

Travis's eyes narrowed. "He working close?"

"All I know is he and the men will be home for lunch around noon."

His bloodshot eyes moved to the clock. "That's an hour. I'll wait down here."

He continued down the stairs, grimacing with every step.

Alex and Claire exchanged puzzled looks.

"Travis, you've been acting like a bear woke up on Christmas Day ever since you came to at the hospital," his sister pointed out, hands on her hips. "What's wrong?"

He stopped and stared up at her a long minute, then descended to the next step. "I'll be on the porch."

Alex sighed. "Can I get you anything?"

"No."

She shook her head and returned to the kitchen, determined to ignore him. Claire followed.

"A good night's sleep didn't do him any good, did it?" the girl said.

"At least he seems clearheaded."

Claire harrumphed. "But it's not an improvement. Is it lunchtime already? I thought I was heading down for breakfast."

"You want something now or are you going to wait?" Alex asked.

"I'll wait. Let me go get dressed, then I'll come down and help you."

"Thanks."

As Alex worked on lunch, she could hear the porch swing squeak slowly. It didn't take a genius to figure out that something Hank had done or said was eating at Travis. Hank had left early, before Travis woke up, so he didn't have a chance to learn what was bothering his brother. Now it looked like Travis came down determined to have it out. Knowing Hank's mule-headedness and temper, and having had this glimpse into Travis's, she hoped she wasn't anywhere around when it happened. Maybe she could head them off until after lunch.

Claire joined her twenty minutes later. Together they started cooking enough hamburgers to feed the troops while Alex kept a watch for Hank. Halfway through, she saw him striding across the yard.

"There he is," she told Claire. She didn't have to say who. Alex hurried to the screen door, Claire not far behind.

Travis didn't get up as Hank stepped onto the porch.

"What are you doing out of bed?" Hank demanded.

"Go to hell, big brother."

Hank stiffened.

"Travis!" Claire exclaimed.

"Hank—" Alex began.

Hank cut her off with a chopping motion of his hand. "I've had a bellyful of my little brother's fits." He pointed a finger at Travis. "You've been a jackass since the minute we walked into your hospital room. If it's the pain—"

"It's not the pain."

"Then what the hell is it? I demand to know why you're treating me and Claire and Alex like something you stepped in at the barn."

"Oh, you *demand* to know, do you?"

"Damn straight."

Travis rose with a grimace of pain. "Hank, the great communicator, demands an answer. He has to know why I'm being such a jerk. Why should I tell you anything? You never return the favor."

"What the hell are you talking about?"

"I'm talking about a conversation I had with Ruff Lewis. You don't know him, do you? He's the foreman at the Box Seven south of Winslow, Arizona. It's owned by a Japanese firm. He wanted to know more about the sale of the Garden. Seems his company is planning to put a bid on it."

Alex covered a gasp with her hand. She felt Claire stiffen beside her.

Travis took a menacing step forward. "Is it true, big brother? Is the Garden up for sale?"

Hank stared at his brother a long moment, then glanced at Alex and Claire. "I would've called you by now if you hadn't gotten hurt. Now that you're here we can discuss it face-to-face." He ran a hand down his jaw. "We have to sell the Garden."

# Chapter Ten

As Claire cried, "No!" Alex stumbled through the door. She faced Hank, willing him to take back his words.

He stared at her, his eyes unblinking, unreadable.

Travis took another stiff step toward his brother. "When were you going to tell us? When you wanted our signatures on the papers?"

Hank grabbed his hat off with one hand and ran the other through his hair. "Things aren't final yet, but we've got to decide soon. I told the agent I'd get back to him after I talked to you. Ruff's Japanese firm has the highest offer." He told them exactly how much it was.

Travis cussed, Claire gasped and Alex glanced at the three Edens. So much money. How could they refuse? But how could anyone put a price on their home?

"That's an awful lot of money," Claire said. "But where would we live?"

"You'll have enough money to get a place while you go to college," Hank said. "And you can afford to go anywhere you like, not just a state university."

Travis walked to the edge of the porch and looked out over the ranch. "Grandpa Henry must be turning over in his grave.

Dad, too. Edens have lived on this land for a hundred years, and you want us to sell out.'' He turned to face his brother. ''You've broken the barrier string this time, Hank. I'm not selling a single rock on this ranch.''

''Then tell me how we keep it.''

Travis was silent a long minute. ''What the hell are you talking about? The Garden isn't in financial trouble. You brought us out of debt years ago.''

''And the politicians are working to put us right back in. I'm talking about property taxes, little brother. You don't stay in one place long enough to have ever heard of them, but they're killing the Garden. They rose seventy-five percent last year alone. Looks like they'll rise again this year. Ranches have gone under all over Wind River Valley, one by one. Looks like ours is next.''

Alex felt like the world was being ripped from beneath her. What she thought was solid ground suddenly shifted, leaving her drifting in space. She thought she'd found the home she'd been searching for all her life. The Garden seemed so permanent. Edens had been living on the ranch for nearly a hundred years. She'd been certain they'd be there for a hundred more. Her feelings for Hank were so mixed up with her love for the Garden that she didn't know if she loved the man or the ranch.

Suddenly the difference seemed important.

''The hell ours is next,'' Travis replied, drawing her attention back.

''Then tell me how we keep it,'' Hank roared. ''I've been tearing my hair out for three years now, trying to figure it out. I can't see any options.''

''There are always options,'' Travis said.

''Give me one.''

''How much are the taxes?''

Hank named a sum that made Alex's heart plummet. She'd had no idea it cost so much to maintain a ranch. And that was just one expense.

''I can cover that,'' Travis said without blinking. ''I've got enough winnings saved up to—''

"No," Hank said flatly. "I'm not taking your money."

Travis's eyes narrowed. "You don't have any choice, big brother. You only own one-third of this ranch. You may control Claire's share, but not mine. I will pay the damn taxes, and there's nothing you can do to stop me."

Hank released a deep, frustrated breath. "Okay, say you pay them this year. Say you pay them next year and the year after that. Even as much money as you make on the circuit, you'll soon run out."

"I'll get a job instead of going to the university," Claire offered, finally speaking up.

"No!" her brothers thundered in chorus.

Claire backed up a step at their vehemence. "But I could help—"

"You can help by graduating and getting a good job," Travis told her. "We've got the short-term solution down. We need to think of long-term now."

"But Hank said—"

"He doesn't want to take my money because he thinks losing the ranch is his fault. He thinks it means he's failed. That he's let down our father and grandfather and great-grandfather." Travis met Hank's eyes squarely, daring him to deny it.

Hank was good at hiding his feelings, but not from Alex. Not anymore. She saw the pain clearly in the tightening of his lips, the muscle that twitched along his jaw. The wound Travis rubbed salt into wasn't fresh, but it had been picked at a lot, and recently. Hank blamed himself for losing the Garden.

Suddenly Alex knew how she felt—disappointed. And angry at Hank for not telling her or his siblings anything about his plans. But there wasn't the soul-deep sense of loss that should have been there if the Garden was so vital to her happiness.

Visions of the only home she'd ever known swept across her mind. She could see the house on Magnolia Street plainly even now. White frame with a high pitched roof, it had a deep, wide porch that ran around the front and sides. She could see the corner of the kitchen where she played with her doll listening to her mother hum as she cooked. Her mother's big bed where she would run to safe, warm arms when something scared her in the night. The deep, cool porch where she and her mother would sit on hot summer evenings, watching the fireflies light up the night.

Her mother. All the memories of that home were tied to her mother. It was her mother who made that old house a home, not the walls.

At times the Garden seemed a larger version of the house she'd lived in with her mother. Alex had worked hard to make it shine, just like she and her mother did with their old house, with wax and elbow grease and love.

But all that work hadn't made the Garden hers, and it never would. What made it hers were the people who lived there—Claire and Travis and Hank. Most of all Hank.

She knew now that her plan would never have worked. She couldn't make a home without filling it with people she loved, people who loved her.

Hank was her home, not the Garden.

She loved Hank. If she hadn't been sure of it before, she was absolutely, positively certain now. An enormous weight lifted from her heart, and she forced her mind back to the argument as Travis continued.

"But it isn't your fault, Hank," the younger brother insisted. "Ranches are failing all over the country. The ones that survive are the ones that get creative in their thinking."

"Like what?" Hank demanded. "The price of beef hasn't risen in years, but the costs of raising cattle sure has. So adding to the herd will only make it worse."

"Then let's cut the herd." Travis held up a hand to stop Hank from interrupting. "Hear me out. We can raise fewer cows and concentrate more on rodeo stock. The roping horses you train are getting a reputation nationwide. Hell, nine have gone to the National Finals in the past seven years. Cowboys ask me about your stock everywhere I go. We could probably sell four times as many as we do. We could expand that into a real business. Advertise. Hire a few more hands to help. Go to major shows."

A light went on in Hank's eyes. "Think we could earn enough money?"

"Hell, yes. Rodeo's getting bigger every day, getting more professional, more specialized. In order to win, cowboys have to have horses trained by experts. They sure can't train them themselves, not and be on the road three hundred and fifty days out of the year."

Hank rubbed his chin. "You might just have something there."

"Couldn't we sell off part of the Garden if worse came to worst?" Claire asked. "The couple of hundred acres along the Wind River would probably bring as much as the rest of it combined. They've been building a lot of houses along the river in the past few years."

Travis shook his head. "I don't want to give up a single tree. I suppose that's an option if there isn't any other way, but I think training rodeo stock is our best plan. What do you think, Hank?"

Hank took hard looks at all three of them. Then his eyes shifted out to the land in question. Finally he said, "We need to talk about it some more, but I think it just might work."

An audible sigh escaped Travis and Claire. Alex felt like her bones were melting into the porch. She'd faced the devil inside her and stared him down. She knew exactly what she wanted to do with the rest of her life, where she wanted to be. She couldn't wait to tell Hank. But now was not the time. Maybe after lunch—

"Lunch!"

She spun around and raced into the kitchen. Behind her, she heard Travis suggest they move their discussion into the house, but she was too busy saving the hamburgers to care. When she'd rescued the ones in the pan and added another batch, she turned to find Claire and Travis watching her.

"Where's Hank?" she asked.

"He's upstairs getting cleaned up for lunch," Travis told her.

"What do you think about all this?" Claire asked quietly.

Alex thought about that for a minute, then said, "As long

as we're together as a family, I don't care where we live. But I have to admit I'm glad we're staying."

Claire's face lit up. "Then you're going to stay?"

"If Hank wants me."

"I don't think you have to worry about that," Travis said with a grin. "In fact, I think you'd have to stick a knife in his heart to get away from him."

Alex smiled her thanks. "Why don't you sit down in here? That way when you continue the discussion I can hear what you say and finish lunch at the same time."

Travis settled into a chair at the kitchen table but Claire pulled a stack of plates from the cabinet. The burgers in the pan began to sizzle as Travis rubbed his shoulder thoughtfully.

"What I want to know," Claire began as she set the plates on the table, "is what Hank was planning to do after he sold the ranch."

Travis shrugged. "I guess he planned to get a job."

"Right," Claire scoffed. "Can you see Hank working for anybody else?"

Their banter jarred Alex's memory and words Hank said at the rodeo dance in Lander came back to her. As she realized their significance, her heart skipped a beat and she froze with salt upended over the pan.

Travis shrugged. "He could be foreman on a big spread. That—"

"I know what he planned to do." Alex realized she was making a salt lick out of one of the burgers and set the shaker beside the stove. She turned to find their eyes on her. She swallowed with difficulty. "Rodeo."

"Rodeo?" Claire cried.

"Are you sure?" Travis asked.

Alex nodded. She leaned heavily against the counter as pieces of the puzzle that made up Hank Eden fell into place. As each piece fit, her happiness melted like snow swept by a warm Chinook wind. She'd thought he'd learned how to communicate, that he was opening up, letting her and his family know what was going on. He hadn't learned a damned thing. The news about selling the ranch told her that. The realization that he'd only told her part of the truth about returning to rodeo made her certain.

"Hank told me he wanted to return to the rodeo. I thought he meant weekend trips, and I...I told him he should go back because he seemed to love it so much. I didn't know he meant full-time."

Travis's eyes widened, then glazed over as if he remembered his own pieces of Hank's puzzle. "Sweet mother of—" He trailed off, staring down at the checkered tablecloth.

Claire looked between them, clearly puzzled by the pall of gloom that had suddenly descended. "So? Now he won't rodeo."

Alex felt like her throat had been tied in knots. "Oh, yes, he will."

"What are you talking about?" the girl cried. "He's going to train horses."

Travis's brows came together. "I suggested that. He didn't. We don't know if he really wants to do it, or if he's agreeing to it just for us."

"But we're not going to sell the ranch now, right? Who else would run it?"

He shook his head slowly. "I don't know. But we have to let him go."

"We have to *make* him go," Alex corrected softly.

Travis lifted sympathetic eyes to hers. "*You* have to make him go."

His words stabbed her. "Me?"

"You're the only one who has the power to do it. I've never seen anyone matter more to him than you."

Alex tried again to swallow the knot in her throat. She remembered what Travis had told her outside the rodeo office in Lander. Marriage and National Finals Rodeo Championships don't mix. Married cowboys who tried to go after a national title usually failed at one or the other.

"I can't do it, Travis. I love him too much."

"Do you love him enough?"

Claire slapped both hands on the table. "Will you please tell me what you two are talking about?"

Travis shifted his gaze to his sister. "Don't you see? He's been aching to get back to the rodeo ever since he left eight years ago."

"Bull hockey!" Claire spat. "He could've gone to any number of rodeos in the past eight years."

"But he couldn't contend for a national title—not and run the ranch, too." Travis's good fist pounded the table. "How could I have been so blind? Why didn't I see this years ago?"

"See what?" Claire cried.

"How he worked so hard at the end of the day, roping cows. I thought he was training horses, but that was just an offshoot. He was keeping in form, for the time when he returned to the arena. Did you know he never let his PRCA card expire? Why would he have kept up that expense unless he was planning on going back?"

Claire looked stunned.

"And the way he'd watch me when I talked about my losses and wins. The way he handled the gold buckle I brought home from the National Finals."

"Was he jealous?" Alex asked.

Travis nodded. "Some, I think, but mostly it was awe. Thinking back on it, I'd say he wanted a championship like a captured wolf wants freedom. He would gnaw off his own leg—or sell the Garden—to get away."

Alex closed her eyes against the tears. "He told me that he didn't compete in local rodeos because if he wasn't the lead steer, the view never changes."

"He's never been the lead steer," Travis said. "He came close, though. When Mama and Dad died, he led in bareback riding by twenty thousand dollars over his nearest competitor. He was third in calf roping."

"Then he had to quit," Alex said softly. "He had to come home and run the ranch."

"And raise us," Travis added.

Claire glanced between them. "Are you saying he's resented us all this time? That he hated running the ranch? I don't believe it."

"He'd bite nails before he'd admit it, but deep down, it had to be there."

"He loves us, Travis," Claire insisted. "And he's done everything he could for the Garden."

"Think about how you felt just a minute ago, Claire," Alex said. "When you offered to get a job instead of going to college, didn't you feel just a tiny bit resentful toward the ranch?"

The girl lifted her chin. "Maybe. But I'd do it in a heartbeat."

"Just like Hank did. He gave up his dream for the ranch," Travis said. "He gave up his dream for us, so we wouldn't have to give up ours. I'd say that means he loves us."

"So why was he going to sell the ranch?"

"He finally saw his chance to have his own dream, too." Travis rubbed the back of his neck. "The taxes were just an excuse. He probably didn't even think past that to the alternatives we've come up with. He wants to rodeo that much."

Quiet descended as they absorbed his words. Numb with shock, Alex turned and began flipping the hamburgers.

She'd told Travis and Claire that she was going to stay, but that was before she realized how much Hank loved the rodeo, how much he'd given up. She had to let him follow his dream. She had to give him up by pretending her dream hadn't changed, by pretending she still wanted to go to San Francisco.

She blinked hard to force back tears of anger and frustration. Damn! Damn! Damn! Damn! Damn! Why did she have to realize what she wanted, just before she lost it? It would've been better not to know.

"Does that mean we have to sell the ranch in order to let Hank rodeo?" Claire asked. "I know I've complained about things here, but it's home. I don't want to see the Garden chopped up into little pieces with condos all over it."

Travis's voice was firm. "I'll run the ranch. I can't rodeo, anyway, for a good six months, maybe more. By that time I'll be into next year's money. Maybe I can find a foreman by then. If not, I'll keep on running it. I've had my go at the big time. It's Hank's turn to have his."

"Who'll train the horses?" Claire asked.

"Me," Travis said. "I always have to polish them up, anyway, once Hank hands them over to me. Competition is different from working in an isolated arena. 'Course the hands will help me like they help him."

Claire sighed. "So, this is one of those times when you love someone enough to let them go?"

"Looks like it, kiddo."

The grandfather clock in the hall chimed twelve times before Claire said softly, "Now I understand what you were talking about earlier. Alex, what are you going to do?"

Alex turned to face them with as brave a smile as she could manage. "What I have to do. Let him go."

"What if he doesn't want to be let go?" the girl asked.

Alex shrugged. Her shoulder felt like it weighed a ton. "If he doesn't go, he'll regret it. Maybe not now, but someday he would. I don't think he'd blame me, but I would blame myself. He told me he'd rather be sorry for something he's done than for something he didn't do. He said he's lived by that motto all his life." She drew a halting breath. "He has to go."

"Can't you go with him?

Alex shook her head. "He doesn't need me on the road. He'll have enough to think about without—"

"He's coming." Travis's words drew all eyes to the doorway.

Alex's heart pounded with dread. It echoed Hank's footsteps as he walked through the dining room. Then he pushed open the swinging doors into the kitchen and glanced around. His eyes came to rest on her.

Her own stung with tears. To hide them, she turned to face the stove. What she'd learned about this man during the past half hour made her love for him grow beyond any boundaries she knew existed. Even as she realized he didn't love her enough to tell her about his plans to leave.

He gently turned her around to face him. "What's wrong?"

"You were going to sell the Garden. I thought I was about to…to…"

"To lose another home. Right?"

She nodded, hoping he would blame the bleakness of her face on that.

"But we don't have to sell the Garden now." Hank glanced at Travis over his shoulder. "We've got it all figured out, right?"

"You've got that right, big brother. I figure I'll stick around and run the Garden while you rodeo."

For a full minute the only sound in the kitchen was the sizzling of the burgers. Alex tried not to shiver as Hank searched Travis's face, then Claire's, then her's. Why did she feel like she was about to cut his throat when she couldn't even breathe through her own?

He leaned one hip against the counter and crossed his arms over his chest. "Sounds like you three have been doing some talking."

"Since you want to rodeo, that's what you're gonna do," Travis said, his face and voice firm.

"And just who says I want to rodeo?"

"You did," Alex told him. "In Lander. You told me you want to get back to it. I thought you meant on weekends, but you meant full time, didn't you?"

"That's when I thought we were losing the Garden. Now, I—"

"Now what?" Travis's chair scraped the floor. "You've been dying to get back to the rodeo since you left eight years ago. Here's your chance. Go."

Hank's eyes narrowed. "You *have* been doing some talking."

"We just want you to be happy, Hank," Claire said. "If you—"

Travis cut across his sister's words. "You've had the Garden for eight years. It's my turn."

"You think you can do a better job?" Hank growled. "What experience do you have running a ranch? What makes you think you can save it when I couldn't?"

"I know I have enough saved up to keep it running for the next ten years if we don't sell another steer," Travis told him. "And if you don't like it, I'll buy you out."

They glared at each other across the room. Alex wanted to throw herself between them, but she couldn't. Travis knew his brother well. Talking about Hank's sacrifices would only make him dig in his heels.

"No. If anybody's staying at the ranch, it's me." Hank placed an arm around Alex's waist and drew her against him.

She could feel the tension in his hard body, and she wanted to wrap her arms around him to show her support. But that's the last thing she could do.

"Why?" Alex asked softly.

He looked down at her, his eyes suddenly tender. "Because I love you, and this is where you'll be happy."

She felt like every knife in the kitchen just flung itself into her heart. He loved her? How could he tell her this now?

She pushed away from him and fled to the other side of the kitchen. "No! You can't use me as an excuse to hold you here."

"I don't want to rodeo. Okay, I thought I did for a while, but that was before you came. You made this old house a home, Alex. You made it my home. It never was before you came. It was my father's. I realized that on the trail drive." He took a step toward her but stopped when she took one back. "I just want to be with you. I want to make the Garden your home, too." He held out his arms. "I want to make these your home."

Why didn't he just slice her into pieces? "An hour ago you planned on selling the Garden."

"That was when I thought there was no other way. Now there is. I don't know if we'll be able to keep the Garden for the next fifty years, but Travis's money will help."

"You can send *your* winnings home, big brother."

Hank's fists slammed down on the counter. "I'm not going to rodeo!"

"Yes, you are," Alex insisted.

"You want to spend your life on the road?" he cried. "It's not as great as it sounds. It's fleabag motels, long hours on the road, bad meals—"

"I'm not going with you," she said quietly.

He stared at her, disbelieving. "And just where the hell are you going to be?"

Alex looked at Travis, pleading with her eyes. She didn't want witnesses when she took the knives from her own heart and buried them in Hank. She didn't know how many she'd have to fling to make him leave, but she knew she'd feel every one.

Travis took the hint. "Come on, Claire. They need to be alone."

Claire followed her brother obediently, but paused first to give Alex's hand a squeeze. Alex squeezed back gratefully, then watched them leave.

Hank's eyes stayed on her, but he waited for them to go before insisting, "You're staying at the Garden. You're going to marry me."

The first knife twisted into her own heart. Alex nearly staggered from the pain. She shook her head. "You never asked me to stay. And you certainly never asked me to marry you."

"I told you I needed you," he roared. "What the hell did you think I meant?"

"Words, Hank. People need to hear the words in plain English. You never tell anybody anything, then you expect them to know what's going on."

He closed the distance between them and took her shoulders in his hands. "I was going to ask you the first minute we had alone after the trail drive, then I had to drive to Phoenix. And there hasn't been time since I got home. So I'm asking now. Stay with me, Alex. I love you. I need you. Marry me."

Somehow she kept tears from her eyes. "No. I'm going to San Francisco. That was the plan all along. It hasn't changed."

He jerked as if she'd thrust knife number one between his ribs. "You don't mean that."

"Yes, I do."

"What the hell kind of games have you been playing for the past two weeks then?" His fingers dug into her shoulders. "You all but begged me to ask you to stay at the Garden."

Alex's chin rose at the reminder. "You're right. All this time I thought you were being noble. That you didn't ask because you thought I wanted to go to California. I didn't know you had your own selfish agenda. You didn't ask because you didn't want to be tied down. You were planning on leaving the whole time."

He winced as the truth cut deep. "But I'm not going now."

"Yes, you are." She watched pain and anger play across his face. She hated herself for what she was doing, hated the agony she saw in his eyes.

"Why are you doing this?"

"Because..." What could she say? That she didn't want to look at regret over the breakfast table the rest of her life? That she didn't want to live with guilt for robbing him of a championship he never won? That she wanted all of him or nothing at all? Those arguments wouldn't drive him away.

His hands slid to her arms and tightened. "You love me. I know you do."

Alex's eyes closed against the tears. Did she have the strength to say the words that would make him leave?

How could she? The anguish threatening to overwhelm her was ten times worse than when she held her mother's hand and watched her fade away. Her mother never came back. Hank probably wouldn't, either.

Her fingernails dug into her palms.

She had to find the strength somewhere. She couldn't tie him down, not to her, not to the Garden. Like Claire said, she had to let him go because she loved him. Because freedom was the only way he would find his dream. And without his dream, he'd never be happy. She'd never be happy.

With a shaking, shallow breath, she looked him square in the eyes. "How could I love a man who would sell his family's home without even telling them it was up for sale? A man who knows how much having a home and family means to me, but is so closemouthed he wouldn't tell me he's giving up his own home to chase a gold buckle? How can I ever trust you after this?"

His startled expression told Alex her knives had sunk deep. His grip tightened. "Alex, I swear I've learned my lesson.

From now on, I'll tell you when I'm going to breathe. Just don't leave me.''

She felt as if her own blood flowed from the wounds she'd dealt him, but she had to go in for the kill. ''You haven't learned a damn thing. But I have. You've kept me from making a big mistake, Hank, and I guess I should thank you for that. You've made me realize it's not you that I love, it's the Garden.''

Hank had to lock his knees to keep them from buckling. He shook his head, as much to clear it as to negate her words. ''I don't believe you.''

Alex pulled her hands from his grip and wrapped her arms around her waist, as if to protect herself from him. ''I didn't realize it until you said were going to sell the ranch. My first thought was that there wasn't anything here for me anymore. I guess I've been in love with the idea of this wonderful place being my home.''

Every muscle in his body stiffened to keep from roaring with the pain raging through him. Alex didn't love him?

''Why?'' he growled.

She hugged herself tighter. ''Why what?''

''Why did you make me think you loved me?''

She winced and cast her eyes at some point behind him. ''I'm sorry.''

''That's all you can say?'' For every step he took toward her, she took one back, so he stopped.

''Go to the rodeo, Hank. You won't be happy unless you do.''

Happy? Didn't she know he couldn't be happy without her? Just the thought of waking up every morning without the hope of seeing her, without talking to her, without kissing her, made him want to howl like a lone wolf.

How could this be happening? He had played by her rules. He'd opened up and shared his feelings with her. Okay, he'd left out one detail, but for that she has to rip his heart out and stomp on it like it was a bug trying to invade her kitchen?

How could he leave her? He didn't want to rodeo anymore.

He wanted to stay home with Alex. And that home—their home—was the Garden.

He spun on his heel and raked a hand through his hair. But how could he stay if she wasn't going to be here? Her ghost would haunt the Garden. He'd walk in the door expecting to see those golden eyes light up, but they wouldn't be around.

Being here every day without her would kill him.

He strode to the kitchen door and turned to face her, feeling empty and utterly without hope. "I'll leave in the morning."

She nodded curtly. "Me, too."

# Chapter Eleven

*W*hump.

Hank's back slammed into the dirt. He struggled to draw breath into his shell-shocked lungs as Jackhammer bucked and kicked his way on down the arena.

"Hot dang, folks! Wasn't that a beaut of a bronc ride? It was close, but the judges say this cowboy made eight seconds before ol' Jack hammered him off! We'll get a score in just a minute!"

Hank's lungs sucked in air a split second before three ugly faces cut off his vision of the dark Texas sky.

"You okay, son?" asked an old codger.

Another squatted beside him. "We gonna need the stretcher?"

The rodeo clown leaned over him. "See if he knows what his name is."

Every muscle in his body screamed in protest, but Hank sat up to satisfy them. "Hell."

"He says his name is Hell!" the clown called back to the cowboys lining the deck of the chutes.

The crowd caught the joke, and a relieved laugh traveled around the arena. Applause and cheers followed as Hank stood and shrugged off the support the old codger offered him.

"Credit Hank Eden with a score of eighty-two!" the announcer proclaimed. "First place!"

Hank staggered over to the fence and leaned against it. First place. Hell.

The crowd renewed their cheers, but Hank barely heard them. After two months of riding and roping from Montana to Texas, he couldn't tell a hoot from a holler, and could care less.

Had he gotten old, or had he just forgotten how hard life on the rodeo circuit was? The life of a rodeo hand was hell. Pure and simple. The only part he didn't hate was being on the back of a bronc or a roping horse, chasing a steer or calf down the arena. But that lasted only a few seconds a day.

Every joint in his body ached, especially his old knee injury. Every muscle screamed in protest every time he lifted himself onto his roping horse. The few brain cells he had left cried "Go home!" every time he dropped onto the bare back of a bronc.

Hank's gaze fell on the gate. The call of home was so strong tonight he could taste it on the wind. Before he knew what he was doing, he'd taken several steps toward the exit.

He forced himself to stop. How could he go home? Though her body was in California, a piece of Alex would remain in every corner of the Garden. He'd hear the echo of her laugh every time he passed Maisy's stall. He'd walk in the back door at night and expect to smell her cooking. He'd sit on the porch swing and want to draw her warmth against him. And he'd remember the pain of her words stabbing through him.

*It's not you that I love. It's the Garden.*

Pain stabbed Hank anew, like a pitchfork driving into his chest.

So why not go home? Would he hurt any more at the Garden than he did now? He didn't see how that was possible, not and go on living. At the Garden he'd have the comfort of home surrounding him. At least she'd given him that. He'd have his family and his work and that would be enough...until the pain went away.

Hank pulled open the exit gate. To hell with rodeo. To hell with gold buckles. He was going home to stay.

Travis and Claire would probably give him grief, but he

didn't care. He'd just sit on the swing and ignore them until they gave up.

He stopped in mid-stride.

Hell no, he wouldn't ignore them. He'd sit his brother and sister down on that swing and tell them exactly what he thought about them forcing him to leave.

Smiling in anticipation, Hank hitched the horse trailer and loaded his two roping horses. Then he climbed in the truck and cranked up the engine. Nine-thirty. If he drove straight through, he would make it home by morning.


"Travis? Claire? Anybody home?" Hank called as he shed his hat and boots in the mud room.

No answer, but he didn't expect there to be. Claire was probably at her summer job and Travis out with the cattle. He could get a few hours sleep before he had to face them.

But first a bite to eat. He wrinkled his nose as he stepped into the kitchen. The odor of Claire's cooking lingered heavy in the air.

The memory of Alex standing by the stove, greeting him with a smile and the heavenly scent of pot roast, stopped him dead in his tracks. But he pushed through the pain and walked over to the cabinet by the phone where the peanut butter was kept. Why hadn't Travis hired a decent cook?

A red light blinking on the counter caught his eye. So that was the damned answering machine he'd gotten every other time he'd called home.

Hank studied it a minute, then pushed a button labeled Playback and after a loud tone, a male voice said, "This is Matt Duvall from Henryetta, Oklahoma. Got a check on a heelin' mare your brother Hank lent me down in Fort Smith and wondered could I buy her. On the road most days. You know how it is. I check my messages, though." Matt left his number.

Hank pulled the peanut butter from the cabinet. He remembered Matt. The Oklahoma cowboy had a good ride that night. He'd call him later.

After another loud beep, Keith Pascall down at the feed store told Travis the vaccine he ordered was in.

Hank reached for the bread and began spreading the peanut

butter. This machine was mighty convenient. Maybe he should've listened to Travis years ago when he wanted Hank to buy one. He had to admit it had been nice to leave messages when he called with some instruction about the ranch he'd forgotten to give Travis, instead of having to call back until his brother was home. It had been nice to hear Claire's voice tell him to leave a message, even if he couldn't talk to her. He'd ended up calling several times a week, and now he knew why. He wanted to come home.

After another loud beep Mallory Hughes told Claire to call when she got home. Hank smiled at a tidbit Mallory added about the boy she was dating. He lifted his sandwich as the next message began.

"Travis? Claire? You there?"

Hank froze. It was Alex. He'd recognize that sweet Southern drawl the rest of his life.

"I guess I missed you again. I can't get used to Pacific time."

Again? She'd called before? Why the hell—?

"Just calling to get my semi-weekly report on how Hank's doing. Gosh, I miss you guys. Well, I'll call later when I know you're home. 'Bye."

Hank's heart hammered in his chest.

The machine beeped again, then whirred, clicked and finally stopped.

Hank stared at it as if he could see through the phone wires. Then he dropped his sandwich and pressed Playback again. Did she say what he thought she said? She'd been calling several times a week to see how he was doing in the rodeo?

Uncertain how to fast forward, he had to listen through the first three messages before he came to hers. Yep, that was exactly what she said. Why would she do that unless she cared more than she'd let on? A helluva lot more.

The back door opened, and Travis appeared in the kitchen doorway. "What are you doing home? I thought you were headed to New Mexico this week."

Hank glared across the room. "How long has she been calling?"

To his credit, Travis didn't pretend not to know who he was

talking about. His gaze fell to the answering machine. "Didn't think you'd know how to work the damn thing."

"Wasn't hard to figure out," Hank growled. "How long?"

Travis met his gaze squarely. "She called as soon as she arrived in San Francisco. She's been calling a couple of times a week. I think Claire calls her some, too."

"Why?"

He shrugged. "To check up on us."

"When she left, she made it clear she didn't give a damn about us. She said she just loved the Garden."

A muscle twitched in his brother's left cheek. "She said she didn't give a damn about you, not us."

Hank's eyes narrowed. "Then why is she so interested in my scores?"

Travis cussed and threw a dirty look at the answering machine. He searched Hank's eyes a long moment, then pulled a hand along his jaw. He spun about and strode to the sink to fill a glass with water. "Why are you home?"

"I came home for good. Now answer my question."

Travis looked at him in surprise. "What do you mean for good?"

"I mean I'm sick of rodeo so I came home. Now why is Alex calling?"

"What about the National Finals? What about the gold buckle you've always—"

"To hell with gold buckles!" Hank slammed both fists on the kitchen table. "You can be the Edens' Gold Buckle Cowboy. I'm too old for the rodeo circuit, or too smart. Either way, I'm staying home and taking care of the Garden. Now if you don't tell me why Alex has been calling, I'm going to—"

"Do you mean it? You're home to stay?"

"Of course I mean it. I always mean—"

"'What I say,'" Travis finished for him. He took a long swallow of water. "I remember."

"Travis, I swear—"

"She loves you."

The words stopped Hank like a brick wall. Breathing, pulse, brain activity—all bodily functions shut down until the meaning penetrated. Then everything went into overdrive. Hope swept through him like a brush fire, but he quickly stamped it out. "She told me she didn't."

"She lied."

Hank stared at his brother, unable to comprehend. "Why the hell would she do that?"

"To make you leave. To send you back to the rodeo."

Hank leaned forward on the table, afraid his knees were going to give out. "And you let her."

"Hell, I helped her. So did Claire."

The only reason Hank didn't rush across the kitchen and put a dent in Travis's square jaw was because he wanted information from him. "I don't believe it."

"It's true. You'd done enough sacrificing for us, Hank. We wanted to give something back."

"So you kick me out of my home and send away the only woman I've ever loved. How can I ever thank you?"

Travis looked away at Hank's sarcasm. He set his glass on the counter. "Sounds downright mean when you put it like that. But we meant it as a kindness."

Hank plowed a hand back through his hair. "Maybe. But your kindness nearly killed me."

"It nearly killed Alex, too, but she loved you enough to let you go. She knew you'd never be happy until you got what you've wanted all your life."

"I wanted her," Hank growled. "And I'm going to have her."

Travis grinned in obvious relief. "You going to go get her? Good. She hates working for that uppity Frenchman."

"Jackson Airport into its summer schedule?"

His brother nodded.

"Then there's a flight to Boise in a couple of hours. If I time it just right I can make it to that restaurant before it closes. Do you have the address?"

"Yep. Want me to drive you to Jackson?"

Hank shook his head as he started upstairs to take a quick shower. "I think you've done enough, little brother."

*"Non! Non! Non!"* Etienne Buchaude threw his hands into the air. "You do not julienne carrots with a paring knife."

The master chef jerked the small knife from Alex's hand and gave her one with a long, thin blade. *"Voici."*

Alex forced herself to smile at the pompous little Frenchman. "Merci, Monsieur Buchaude."

He smiled haughtily, like a king with a scullery maid. "You're learning, Alexandra."

Afraid if she smiled at him another second she'd use the knife to julienne more than carrots, Alex returned her attention to the vegetables. She hated the way he used her full name. She hated the way he blew into the kitchen, criticized everything everyone was doing, then stormed out, muttering in French. Like he was doing now.

She wished she'd never heard of Etienne Buchaude or his restaurant. She wanted to be back in Wyoming, where the people appreciated her cooking. And didn't give a damn which knife she used to cut carrots.

Misery rushed in, like it always did when she thought about the Garden, which was at least a hundred times a day. Would the pain ever go away?

She took a deep breath and pushed the memories to the back of her mind.

Here no one appreciated her cooking. She never even saw the customers. She was stuck in the back of the kitchen from four until eleven every evening except Mondays.

Alex sighed, glanced at her boss's retreating back, then put down the long, thin knife and picked up the paring knife. It gave her more control. She wasn't going to slice her fingers for anybody, much less an egomaniac like—

A commotion at the swinging doors scattered her thoughts. Was a customer trying to get into the kitchen? She craned her neck to see around the other chefs wearing white aprons and tall hats. Whoever it was picked a bad time to try it. Monsieur Buchaude forbade anybody but staff in his kitchen. Even now he was rushing over to—

Was that a cowboy hat?

The brief glimpse was snatched away as the master chef thrust himself into the crowd of waiters, busboys and chefs trying to push the intruder out.

Alex shook her head. She was hallucinating. It was just

wishful thinking. Even if it were a cowboy hat, millions of people wore—

"Alex, where the hell are you?"

The shout penetrated every cell in her body. Hank. She'd recognize his bellow anywhere.

The group surrounding him stopped struggling and turned as one to stare at her. But their curiosity barely registered.

Hank was here. How?... Why?...

Her heart performed somersaults in her chest.

Monsieur Buchaude glowered at her. "This is your fault, Alexandra?"

"Let me pass." Hank shoved through the restaurant workers. He stopped as soon as he saw her. His blue eyes bored into hers. "Alex."

"Hank," she whispered. Then she gathered her wits. "What are you doing here?"

Hank strode forward, put an arm behind her knees and swept her into his arms. "I came to take you home."

Alex's arms flew around his neck. Home. The word burned through her like strong liquor—warm, sweet, comforting. Oh, how she'd missed him.

He turned to leave, but the doors were blocked by Monsieur Buchaude.

"What is the meaning of this, Alexandra?"

"I don't know, Monsieur Buchaude. I—"

"She quits," Hank said, then strode forward. "Out of my way, little man."

The chef scooted out of the way shouting curses in his native tongue.

As Hank shouldered the swinging doors open, Alex kicked her feet hard. "What do you think you're doing, Hank Eden? Let me down this instant."

"Hell, no." He threaded his way through tables of richly dressed, gaping patrons.

Alex only stopped kicking when her foot sent a woman's rhinestone and feather hat flying off her carefully coifed hair. Her face flaming, Alex buried her face against his neck. "Damn you, Hank Eden. You'll pay for this!"

He placed his mouth against her ear and murmured, "Promise?"

His warm breath made Alex's head suddenly light. As the restaurant receded from her mind, she closed her eyes and tightened her hold. She felt his heart pounding against her cheek and inhaled his familiar scent. Her own heart hammered in reply. These strong arms felt like home. She took a deep breath, savoring the moments wrapped in his warmth.

Reality intruded when he set her on her feet. They were in the parking lot of the exclusive restaurant, beside a rented black sport vehicle.

Hank reached into his pocket for keys.

Alex yanked the tall, poufy chef's hat from her head and backed away. "Are you out of your mind? I'm not going anywhere with you."

"Oh, yes, you are. I told you, I'm taking you home."

She planted her hands on her hips. "What makes you think you can waltz in here and carry me out like a sack of feed?"

He gave up trying to find the right key and spun to face her. "Because you love me."

Her breath caught, and she froze to the pavement. "How do…why do you think that? I told you—"

He took a step toward her. "Why else would you call the Garden several times a week to check on my progress in the rodeo?"

"Claire told you," she said accusingly. "I knew she couldn't keep her—"

"You told me. On the answering machine." He laid his hands on her shoulders. "Admit it, Alex. You missed me."

She stared into his sexy blue eyes. She shouldn't tell him how miserable she'd been for the past two months. Shouldn't let him know how each day was more painful than the last. Shouldn't even hint that she couldn't eat or sleep for worrying about him, that she didn't give a damn about which sauce went with salmon and which with pork tenderloin. But God help her, she didn't have the strength to drive him away again. "Yes, you sorry son of a cross-eyed snake. I missed you. There, I said it. Are you happy—"

Her words were cut off by his lips. Surprise held her stiff for an instant, then she wrapped her arms around him and poured all her love into the kiss.

Hank leaned her against the car and ground his hips into hers.

Alex felt his arousal and nearly wept with frustration. She wanted him so badly she ached. She tore her mouth away. "Stop. Please!"

His head rose a bare inch from hers. He stared down at her, his breathing as labored as her own. "You're right. We can't make love here."

"We can't make love at all." She tried to push him away, but he wouldn't budge.

"Damn it, Alex, don't go cold on me now," he growled. "I've been living through hell the past two months, wanting you. And after that kiss, you can't tell me you haven't wanted me, too."

Alex searched the face that had been haunting her dreams. That's exactly what she should tell him. But she couldn't summon the desire or the strength. "No, I can't tell you that. It would be the biggest lie I ever told."

"Then why are you pushing me away?"

"Because..." She had to swallow to straighten out the knots in her throat. "Because I love you."

He stared at her so long she thought he hadn't heard her quiet words. Then he grabbed her hand and pulled her under one of the parking lot lights.

"What are you doing?"

"I want to see your face." He stopped suddenly and hauled her around to face him. "Say it again."

Restaurant patrons arriving or leaving stared at them, but Alex ignored them. "I love you, Hank Eden."

"More than the Garden?"

"More than the Garden. More than French cooking. More than Sugar. More than anything else in the world."

His eyes blazed with emotion, and his hands tightened on her shoulders. "Even though I'm not too good at telling people what's going on?"

She smiled softly. "You're learning. Claire said you've been calling several times a week, letting them know which rodeo you were headed to next and talking about what Travis is doing with the ranch. She said Travis never even did—"

Her breath caught as Hank suddenly sank to one knee. "What are you doing?"

He pulled her hand against his heart. "Marry me, Alex. I love you, and I want you, and I need you. I always will."

Her heart hammered against her ribs. She wanted to scream "Yes!" at the top of her lungs, but first she had to know. "What about the rodeo? You wanted to win a gold buckle. I don't want to tie you down. I don't want you to look at me one day and know I kept you from going after your dream."

Hank stood and captured her chin. "I am going after my dream. Don't you see? The rodeo was my dream when I was a boy. I just never let it go. You taught me what's really important. The Garden. Claire and Travis. But mostly you. You're my dream, Alex. The dream of a man, not a boy."

Alex's heart raced for the clouds. "Oh, Hank."

"And why the hell does everyone keep telling me what I want?"

"We thought you'd been dying to get back to the rodeo for eight years. Travis thought you resented the Garden and having to raise him and Claire, because you never won a championship. He thought you resented him because of his gold buckle."

Hank looked away, his eyes narrowed. "I reckon maybe there was a little of that in my decision to sell the Garden. Okay, maybe a lot. But just at first. When I finally realized what I'd be giving up if I left, I knew I didn't want to go anywhere."

"And what would you be giving up?" she asked.

He met her gaze squarely. "You. Darlin', you've put me through hell the past two months. I've never been more miserable in my life. Every time a rodeo was over, I just wanted to head home. Then I'd remember you wouldn't be there, so what was the point? I've done nothing but think about you—during the long drives, while I waited for my turn to ride or rope, at night in one fleabag motel after another. Hell, the nights especially. You even haunted my dreams."

"I did?"

"Waking and sleeping." He slipped his arms around her and drew her close. "Marry me, Alex. I want to live with you at the Garden for the rest of our lives. Will you come with me and make it a home for both of us, and for our children and grandchildren?''

Tears sprang to her eyes. She'd finally learned what home was. Home was not the place where you set your dishes. It was not a hearth, but a heart. Hank's heart, and her own, beating together.

She ran her hand lovingly along his jaw. "Yes, I'll marry you...and live with you wherever you want to live. Because wherever you are, that's my Eden."

\*    \*    \*    \*    \*

*And the Garden of Eden*
*continues to flourish!*
*Look for Claire's story*
*in late 1998 or early 1999 as*
*she meets the man of*
*her dreams!*

# DIANA PALMER
# ANN MAJOR
# SUSAN MALLERY

## RETURN TO WHITEHORN

In **April 1998** get ready to catch the bouquet. Join in the excitement as these bestselling authors lead us down the aisle with three heartwarming tales of love and matrimony in Big Sky country.

A very engaged lady is having second thoughts about her intended; a pregnant librarian is wooed by the town bad boy; a cowgirl meets up with her first love. Which Maverick will be the next one to get hitched?

### Available in **April 1998**.

Silhouette's beloved **MONTANA MAVERICKS** returns in Special Edition and Harlequin Historicals starting in February 1998, with brand-new stories from your favorite authors.

Round up these great new stories at your favorite retail outlet.

*Silhouette* ®

# Take 4 bestselling love stories FREE

## a FREE surprise gift!

## Special Limited-time Offer

**Mail to Silhouette Reader Service™**

3010 Walden Avenue
P.O. Box 1867
Buffalo, N.Y. 14240-1867

**YES!** Please send me 4 free Silhouette Romance™ novels and my free surprise gift. Then send me 6 brand-new novels every month, which I will receive months before they appear in bookstores. Bill me at the low price of $2.90 each plus 25¢ delivery and applicable sales tax, if any.* That's the complete price and a savings of over 10% off the cover prices—quite a bargain! I understand that accepting the books and gift places me under no obligation ever to buy any books. I can always return a shipment and cancel at any time. Even if I never buy another book from Silhouette, the 4 free books and the surprise gift are mine to keep forever.

215 SEN CF2P

| | | |
|---|---|---|
| Name | (PLEASE PRINT) | |
| Address | Apt. No. | |
| City | State | Zip |

This offer is limited to one order per household and not valid to present Silhouette Romance™ subscribers. *Terms and prices are subject to change without notice. Sales tax applicable in N.Y.

# ALICIA SCOTT

**Continues the twelve-book series—36 Hours—in March 1998 with Book Nine**

# PARTNERS IN CRIME

The storm was over, and Detective Jack Stryker finally had a prime suspect in Grand Springs' high-profile murder case. But beautiful Josie Reynolds wasn't about to admit to the crime—nor did Jack want her to. He believed in her innocence, and he teamed up with the alluring suspect to prove it. But was he playing it by the book—or merely blinded by love?

For Jack and Josie and *all* the residents of Grand Springs, Colorado, the storm-induced blackout was just the beginning of 36 Hours that changed *everything!* You won't want to miss a single book.

Available at your favorite retail outlet.

# Return to the Towers!

In March
*New York Times* bestselling author

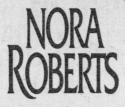

# NORA ROBERTS

brings us to the Calhouns' fabulous
Maine coast mansion and reveals the
tragic secrets hidden there for generations.

For all his degrees, Professor Max Quartermain has a
lot to learn about love—and luscious Lilah Calhoun is
just the woman to teach him. Ex-cop Holt Bradford is
as prickly as a thornbush—until Suzanna Calhoun's
special touch makes love blossom in his heart.
And all of them are caught in the race to solve
the generations-old mystery of a priceless
lost necklace…and a timeless love.

# *Lilah and Suzanna*
## THE
## Calhoun Women

### A special 2-in-1 edition containing
### FOR THE LOVE OF LILAH and
### SUZANNA'S SURRENDER

Available at your favorite retail outlet.

Silhouette®